"The light house"

Jason Luke

Copyright © 2015 Jason Luke

Dedicated to Irene, with love.

Prologue.

The sun spilled the last of its light in a riot of color that glinted across the tops of the waves, as the far-off headland began to distill into the haze of a smudged horizon. High overhead a gull hung on the currents of the wind, its cry like a lost and lonely lament. The crest of a cold green wave rolled relentlessly towards the rocky shoreline – and at that very instant, Connie Dixon took the photo.

The surf detonated around the bleak stark rocks, a sound like thunder that seemed to rumble through the ground beneath her feet. She lifted her face to the heavens as the mist of spray fell pure and soft like pearly rain.

Connie closed her eyes and gave herself over to the vast grandeur of nature – the roar of the surf and the whip of the wind through her hair, as though this isolated piece of Maine coastline could cleanse her troubled soul – wash away the doubts and uncertainties of a life that had become entangled. She felt the cold slap of the breeze and the undulating tug of it like claws at her clothes. She filled her lungs with the crisp sea air and felt the grime and desperation of the city shed from her like a dark heavy coat.

She was shivering – the air was cold and damp, yet standing on the rocky precipice was exhilarating. Her cheeks were flushed, her eyes sparkling. For a moment in time she felt free and awed by the raging vastness of the elements. She tried to cling to that sensation – tried to capture it and immerse herself in the thrill of timeless

3

abandon. Another swell was building out in the ocean, lumpen and round-shouldered until it surged towards the shallowing shore and reared its foaming head majestically. A bluster of wind clawed spume off the crest, and then the wave burst across the rocks below where she stood in an awesome rumble of menacing power.

Connie cupped her hands around the camera and thumbed back through the digital images. She smiled wistfully, as though this fleeting moment was already fading to a memory. The shoreline seemed to hiss and heave as the sea pounded upon it relentlessly. The last sprinkles of sunset finally drained from the fading sky and the gull wheeled away and was lost in the mist. She peered over the face of the cliff, saw the white surf boiling like lava between the craggy jaws of the black rocks, and then shuffled back from the edge as a gusting wind threatened to sway her off her feet.

Connie stood on the lonely promontory until darkness crept across the land and the ocean became a black liquid void of seething sound. She drew a final deep breath of the fresh salt air, hugged herself about the shoulders, then turned her back and walked regretfully from the cliff towards where the rental car was parked.

The trail meandered away from the craggy shore, past a withered wooden bench bleached to the color of anguish and a tin sign, rusted and pitted. Connie felt her steps become heavier. She stood for a moment in the empty parking lot staring up at the first evening stars, and then slid in behind the wheel of the car. The sudden silence was deafening.

There was a film of salty crust across the windshield. Connie started the engine but made no move to drive away. She sat with the motor idling – and then suddenly she began to cry.

She wept with self-pity and despair. She wept for the suffocation her life had become. Soft fat tears rolled down her cheeks and clung like drops of dew to her eyelashes. She heard herself sobbing. She hunched her shoulders and cupped her hands to her face until her misery slowly became anger and impotent loathing. Her hands clenched into tiny fists and she slammed them against the steering wheel in frustration.

"Damn him!" she hissed.

It was all too much – and she had let it happen.

She heard the soft chime of her cell phone and had to resist the instinctive urge to immediately snatch it up. She knew who it was. It was always Duncan.

When she slid the phone from her pocket, she saw three messages from him. Invisible fingers of dread seemed to wrap themselves around her, so that she felt the clutch of them. She opened the phone, read the messages, and shut down without replying. Her hands were trembling with a kind of reckless defiance.

Even here – ten hours from New York, he would not let her go – would not give her peace. His reach was beyond physical; it was an emotional weight of guilt that hung round her neck like a millstone. Yet he had always filled her with emotion, nothing the man ever did was without point or purpose. Duncan dominated the last four years of her life like it was his right, like she was his property.

And she conceded that she was.

She had tried to break away from him in the past, but the man's control was like the intricate web of lies and promises he had woven around her until resisting had seemed exhausting and then impossible. His grip was proprietorial – like a shadowy debt that hung over her, wilting her, weakening her until meek compliance seemed the only way.

Duncan Cartwright was a bastard.

He was affluent and influent – the man who had inherited one of New York's oldest and most venerable commercial art galleries from his aging father, and built the business through ruthless acquisition of works by the world's most prominent artists. He was a charming, debonair man with elegant style and a disarming smile. But behind the mannered, cultivated exterior, his eyes held a secret mockery and challenge. He was a pirate, as lethal and dangerous as a dagger in the dark shadows.

Connie had been a thirty-year-old woman from the Midwest when she had left a futile life behind in Kansas to chase her dream in the Big Apple armed with little more than a few months' rent money, an arts degree and a desperate ambition to paint. Duncan had discovered her at a downtown studio, and set about winning her with the same drive and ruthless determination he used to acquire all the other beautiful trappings he had adorned his flamboyant life with.

He was strikingly good-looking, tall and slim with metallic blonde hair and a flashing white smile. He exuded the mesmerizing allure of a cobra, and Connie had been bewitched. She recalled the day he had first visited her in her little apartment, and felt a slide of secret shame at the sting of that memory.

He had come in the afternoon while she had been working at her easel and he had spoken to her with a passion for her work that had swept her off her feet. It was a powerful performance: he drifted across the floor of her studio with the sun behind him so that he seemed to shine like some ancient god as he talked about her future – and she could not take her eyes from him. Then, when he paused to emphasize a point, she had felt something move within her, and sensed a significant shift behind the man's enigmatic eyes. He had leaned in, his gaze blazing with fervent enthusiasm, and thrust a face that glowed close to hers. He was close enough to kiss, so that she had felt her breath seize in her throat with a giddy excitement that had left her trembling and reckless. He had seen her eyes grow wide and solemn with fear for the thing that she had felt stir deep within her, and he knew then that he had her.

He had promised to support her career. He had promised exhibitions and the chance to be famous. He filled her head with dreams of recognition – and then he had taken her easily to his bed.

It had been a time in Connie's life of illicit passion and wild excitement as she threw herself into her work and gave herself willingly to him in return. It had been a careless interlude that had quickly tarnished with regret.

In the four years since, her dream had died, stolen from her by Duncan's ruthless need to have her – to own her completely. There had been no exhibitions, only slowly mounting debt as he continued to support her until she realized, too late, that he had bought her, body and soul.

She began to work for the gallery, selling the art of other artists during the day, and surrendering herself to Duncan on his whim. She had tried to resist, but he could always bring her back – always manipulate her guilt until the exhaustion and entanglement to the man became suffocating. She had even left the gallery the year before, but he had dragged her back, menaced her with threats to ruin her and have her mother removed from the nursing home.

"You owe me," he had jabbed a finger into her face, his features twisted into a grotesque snarl when she had returned chastened to him because of the burden of paying for her elderly mother's care. "You owe me for everything I have done for you."

Connie smudged the tears from her eyes and sat in the dark silence, her gaze vacant, her eyes haggard and hollow. Outside the car, the wind was rising. She felt the buffet of a gust sway the vehicle on its suspension, and then a swirl of dirt and dust rattled against the windshield. She took a deep breath and glanced at her ghostly reflection in the rearview mirror. Her eyes were red-rimmed, her face pale as alabaster. She set her jaw grimly and then on a sudden impulse, she wound down the car's window and hurled the cell phone defiantly out into the dark night.

"Damn him!" she said again, and then an instant later felt a pang of dread that tasted bitter as regret. She reversed the car before guilt overwhelmed her and turned back onto the highway, headed towards town.

She had come to Maine for two weeks of vacation to escape and to think. She was drowning in despair and debt, living without love, and she sensed that the path of her future was one that would drain the last of life's great mystery from her.

She had come to Maine to make decisions, while they were still hers to make — while she still clutched at the last shreds of her will to be free.

She had come to the sleepy coastal town of Hoyt Harbor looking to find answers, without knowing that fate was about to divert her life onto a blind date with destiny.

1.

Connie woke late in the morning and lay still for a moment while she cast her mind about to remember where she was. Bright sunlight streamed through the curtained window and she could hear the far-off sounds of gulls squabbling above a murmur of traffic noise.

She sat up in the bed and yawned. She had a sense of something lost and gained. She reached instinctively for her phone and then stilled the movement. There was an instant jab of remorse, like the prick of a needle at her conscience, but she shrugged the weight off with a determined sigh and went across the bedroom of the vacation rental to peer through the drapes.

Sprawled below her was the idyllic hamlet of Hoyt Harbor, the narrow streets brimming with the first tide of summer vacationers who were funneling into town across the bridge. The sky was clear and a shattering blue, and the sun through the glass was warm on her cheek. Despite herself, Connie felt an irrepressible lift of pleasure that stayed with her while she showered and dressed and lightened her steps as she strolled down the hill.

The harbor was a bite chewed out of the coastline – a sheltered cove against the storms and gales that swept down from the northeast. It had once been home to a small fishing fleet, but the years had not been kind to the folks of Hoyt Harbor. While other communities up and down the Maine coast had endured, the locals had reluctantly been forced to abandon the industry, and slowly rebuilt a fragile economy on the back of tourist dollars. Yet everywhere were memories of a proud past – gaily painted trawlers nudged at their moorings in the harbor, and the shops along the busy waterfront were decorated in nautical themes while white winged seagulls gathered in raucous clusters on the rocky break wall and squawked at picnicking families for scraps.

Connie went down the gentle slope towards the harbor, her summer dress swishing about her knees, her long dark hair a careless cascade piled atop her head. When she reached the main street into town she thrust a hand into her handbag and pulled out her sunglasses. The sunlight off the placid harbor glinted like liquid gold. She watched for a moment while two young boys wearing bright lifejackets pushed a canoe onto the water, the lilting laugh of their voices ringing clear as a chimed bell to where she stood.

There was an air of excitement – of bubbling urgency in the air, as if the tourists that flocked to the tiny town were unwilling to waste a single moment. Connie felt herself swept up in the atmosphere and smiled without realizing it.

The harbor's waterfront had once been a cobblestone path where fishermen unloaded their catch and trawler nets hung to dry like laundry in the breeze. Now every square inch of space was given over to outdoor café tables and seasonal stallholders who had come to town to sell their wares. Connie drifted aimlessly amongst the stands and smelled the mingled aromas of fresh baking and brewed coffee while harried young waitresses rushed in and out of the restaurants wearing strained smiles, and children ran with balloons and fell tumbling and laughing on the grassy verge.

By midday the crowds along the waterfront were an impenetrable throng. Connie wandered towards the harbor's edge where a wide pier thrust like an accusing finger into the deep water. Over the heads of the crowds she could see a cluster of tourist shops nestled and shaded under wide awnings. A man wearing a white t-shirt and pants, and shoes with no socks, caught her eye. He had a pair of sunglasses perched on top of his carefully groomed hair, lolling indolently in a café chair. He gave her a long slow admiring glance over the top of his newspaper and then arched an eyebrow in a flirted invitation. Connie felt the man's eyes upon her until she stepped across the threshold of the closest shop.

The difference in temperature was dramatic. The air inside the store was air-conditioned and the narrow aisles of cheap tourist gifts were crammed full of t-shirted tourists with pasty white arms and legs. Connie drifted through the store and then stepped back out onto the sidewalk, back into the warm afternoon sun. The other shops were all similar boutiques, and she turned her head and stared into the distance. About a mile from the waterfront there was another dark cluster of buildings on a gentle rise, hunched low to the ground. She started to walk, and then realized there was a door wedged between two of the tourist shops that she hadn't seen. Painted on the glass of the door were the words, 'Hoyt Harbor Gallery and Gifts'.

Gallery.

She stepped back to the edge of the pier and propped her sunglasses on top of her head. She could see a second story to the building that she had assumed were merely commercial offices. She went back towards the glass door and pushed it open.

A narrow set of stairs led up to a white-walled space that had polished wooden floorboards and a collection of local paintings displayed. At the far end of the gallery was a small waist-high glass counter, and behind it a closed door that she presumed would be some kind of storage area. The gallery was deserted, and she heard the hollow echo of her footsteps as she idled past the first few garish oil paintings.

The works on the stark walls were poorly executed harbor paintings, a mixture of abstracts and a rash of vague landscapes. She stepped close to one of the harbor scenes and studied it with a critical eye. The work was on canvas and painted in oils, but she could see the paint had been applied badly and the colors were starkly layered without any feel for the subject or understanding of the craft. She stepped back, glanced forlornly at the rest of the work around her and saw nothing of interest. She was about to turn and leave quietly when she realized there was an alcove at the far end of the gallery – a small ante-room. She heard a murmured voice and out of idle curiosity, went towards the sound.

The gallery was an L shape, and the alcove was just an additional ten square feet of space that might have once been a bathroom before the renovators and painters had remodeled. There were three big watercolors on one wall that Connie dismissed with barely a glance, and on the opposite wall were several small portraits. They were charcoal sketches. The people were all old, their facial features deeply etched, as if they had been the hasty studies of an exuberant local art student.

Connie turned, and then stopped abruptly.

There was another woman in the gallery, blocking her view of the wall ahead of her. The woman was dressed in shorts and a t-shirt. She had thick stumpy legs and was wearing a wide-brimmed straw hat. She was muttering to herself. She sensed Connie behind her and glanced over her shoulder. Her eyes swept over Connie in an instant, and then she arched her eyebrows and grudgingly stepped aside.

Connie gasped.

Set on the wall ahead of her was a painting – a masterpiece so exquisite that Connie felt the shock and awe of it raise the fine hairs along her arms.

For a moment she could not breathe. She felt a hot flush of color blush her cheeks and then an instant of some kind of sensuous vertigo so that she felt herself teeter.

The painting was no larger than her handbag, and yet she saw within it all the intangible elements beyond the craft that accumulated into a painting so beautiful and so powerfully evocative that she felt tears well in her eyes.

It was a seascape set under an ominous brooding sky, with a desolate strip of coastline in the foreground and pounding surf breaking upon black glistening rocks. Tiny – yet somehow perfectly detailed – was the haunting image of a young woman standing in the foreground with her back to the artist so that she seemed to be filled with a yearning and a longing that was almost tragic.

The painting was oil on canvas set within a simple silver frame. Connie went towards the wall, overcome with a sense of reverence. She caressed the frame with the tips of her fingers as if to feel what the artist had felt – as if to connect herself with this wondrous thing of beauty.

She had felt this same profound reaction to a painting only once before in her life. On a month-long vacation in Europe to celebrate her twenty-fifth birthday she had found herself in a gallery. Standing before Vermeer's *'Woman in Blue Reading a Letter'* at the Rijksmuseum, she had wept behind the red velvet rope, for she had never seen a painting that seemed to evoke and capture the sense of timeless sorrow and suffering of every woman who had ever known love.

That moment in Amsterdam had inspired her passion for art and set the course for her future. Now this little painting hanging in a craft gallery on the rugged coast of Maine spoke to her in the same mesmerizing way.

Connie sniffed back tears of deep emotion and wonder. She peered hard at the painting for long fascinated minutes. Every brush stroke was flawless, capturing the movement of the waves, the solitude of the sea, the looming menace of the sky. But it was the girl in the foreground that her eyes kept being drawn back to. She had long dark hair, whipped by the wind, and she was wearing a simple gown that hung to her feet. There was something beseeching in the way the artist had captured the girl – an ethereal quality that transcended mere paint to empower her.

On a reckless impulse, Connie snatched the painting off the wall. She turned the canvas over. It was unsigned. There was nothing on the back of the painting and somehow she felt cheated and disbelieving. She carried the painting to a light on the wall and peered closely at the edges. There was no mark, no signature. She felt the air escape her in a desperate sigh of disappointment.

Yet she was trembling, filled with a growing sense of incredulity. A swirl of superstitious nausea washed through Connie as she stared hard at the painting. She felt a preternatural chill turn her blood to ice. She began to shake with dawning realization of what this was – of who had crafted this masterpiece, and the thrill of that was an incredulous tingle of disbelief and giddy joy.

She tucked the painting under her arm and thrust her hand deep into her bag – then remembered she no longer had her phone. She went quickly to the glass counter. There was a phone on the wall. Connie snatched it up and realized her hands were shaking.

Suddenly the door behind the counter swung violently open and a middle-aged woman came into the gallery. There was a look of horror and alarm on her face. She glared at Connie and her mouth gaped open.

"What are you doing?" the woman rasped.

Connie froze for an instant. The woman's eyes were wide with shock. She saw the painting wedged under Connie's arm and she snatched at it. Connie dropped the phone and took the woman's wrist.

"You have to tell me who painted this," she demanded. Her eyes were wide and glittering, her expression twisted and desperate. "I need to know who the artist is!"

The woman set her jaw into a grim snarl of outrage and reefed the little painting out of Connie's hands. Connie felt a sudden sense of bereft despair as though even to be parted from it for a single moment was an agony.

She took a deep breath, but the hectic desperation stayed in her eyes and put jagged edges to her words. She still had a grip on the woman's wrist and Connie pulled the lady to her and pressed her face close. "Tell me," she insisted. "How did you get this painting? Who is the artist?"

The storage door behind them opened again and an elderly man with bright sparkling eyes set within a weathered wrinkled face stepped into the room. He was scowling with annoyance. The man had spectacles hung from a cord around his neck. He perched the glasses on the end of his nose and stared hard at Connie like she was something extraordinary that he had never seen the likes of before. The man ran his hand through the remaining grey wisps of his hair and sucked his teeth thoughtfully.

"My wife is right, missy," the man said at last. "You can't just go taking paintings off the walls. It ain't proper. Especially not that one." The man pointed at the painting and everyone's eyes went back to the remarkable canvas in his wife's white-knuckled hands.

Connie flinched — and then the breath went out of her in a slow sigh. She seemed to deflate. Her shoulders slumped, the wildness went slowly from her eyes in a moment of sudden realization. She blinked at the man like she was waking from a dream.

"So sorry," she said softly. She shook her head in bewilderment now that the reckless impulse of emotion had cooled. "I... I really don't know what came over me." She tried a disarming smile that hung lopsided from her lips. The man's wife narrowed her eyes suspiciously and set the painting down on the counter — well out of Connie's reach. She looked up at her husband. "Do you want me to call Buck, or one of the deputies?"

The elderly man rocked on the balls of his feet for a thoughtful moment and took another long appraising look at Connie before he shook his head. "I don't think that will be necessary," he mollified his wife.

"But she was stealing!"

Connie shook her head in mute denial but the man cut across her before she could speak. "Mable, most thieves don't run for a phone, darlin'. They run out the door."

His wife flinched, then folded her arms across her ample bosom in a gesture of defiance. She gave Connie a look of withering malevolence. The man turned his attention back to Connie and kept his voice reasonable.

"Now, do you mind telling us exactly what you were doing?"

Connie looked down at her shoes and wrung her hands. "I wanted to buy this painting," she muttered softly. "Can you tell me how much it is?"

The man shook his head. "It's not for sale," he said.

Connie felt a shock like pain. She stared up into the old man's eyes. "But... I'll pay any price," the edge of desperation came back into her voice and she couldn't help it. She dug frantically into her handbag for her purse. She had a thousand dollars. She threw the money onto the counter like it was confetti. "Please," the word sounded like a plea.

The man gave her a kindly smile of sympathy, and then shook his head again. "I'm sorry," he said. "But it ain't for sale. Not at any price."

"Why?"

The man and woman exchanged brief mysterious glances and for a long moment there was just tense, heavy silence. The man started to give an answer, then he stopped, as if he suddenly remembered that he was on the verge of revealing some private local business that shouldn't be revealed.

"It was a gift," he said abstractly. "It can't be sold."

"A gift to you?"

The man nodded. "That's right. To me and Mable."

"From the artist?"

The man nodded and Connie had an inkling that he was reluctant to be drawn any further on the matter.

"Why did he give you the painting?"

19

"That's none of your business," the old man stiffened visibly and Connie was forced to smile an apology.

"Can you at least tell me who the artist is?"

"Local man," the woman said in a blunt tone to cut the conversation short. There was a flash of vindictive triumph in her eyes so that Connie felt the sting of the words like a slap across her face. "One of our own."

"Oh," Connie's voice dropped and lost its timbre, so that it sounded hollow with disappointment. "Can you tell me his name?"

The old man sighed. "Bill Mason," he said softly.

Connie nodded. For an instant she felt nothing but emptiness and despair. A creeping numbness began to fill her – and then slowly... very slowly, the flame of that thrilling sensation which had overwhelmed her flickered back into fire. She choked back a breath of realization and fought to keep her expression blank, but she could feel a faint heat rising on her cheeks. She dug quickly back into her purse and handed the man one of her business cards. "My name is Connie Dixon," she explained. "And I represent the Cartwright Gallery in New York." The card was beautifully embossed, lettered in gold on thick cream stock. The man took the card and turned it over in his hand. "I am here in Maine looking for new artists to represent," she told the white lie. "Your Mr. Mason seems exceptionally gifted, and I would like to talk to him. Can you perhaps tell me where he lives?"

The man handed the card back to Connie and his expression was made grim by her persistence. "Sorry," he said and shook his head. He planted his big gnarled hands on the top of the glass counter and fixed her with his eyes, his gaze suddenly bleak and steely.

"The painting is not for sale, and I can't tell you where Mr. Mason lives. He's a man who likes his privacy."

Connie sighed. She cast a longing glance at the painting on the counter – and then made a last desperate appeal, searching the old man's eyes for a flicker of understanding. "Can I at least take some photos?"

The man straightened, taken off guard. He rubbed his chin, glanced at his wife, then nodded reluctantly. He carried the painting back to the wall and hung it with a special reverence. Connie fetched her camera from her handbag and took a dozen photos, some of the whole painting, then several of the haunting girl in the foreground, and then finally a couple of close-up shots that focused on the artist's unique technique and brushwork. When she was finished she took a deep breath and thanked the man.

"If you want to know anything else, you can try Warren Ryan at the grocery store," the old gallery owner said gruffly. "He might be willing to tell you more."

"Warren Ryan?" Connie frowned with intrigue as she repeated the name. "Are they friends?"

The man shrugged and clenched his jaws. "As friendly as anyone is with Mr. Mason, I suppose," he said mysteriously. "But he might be willing to tell you more, and he might be willing to sell his paintings. You'll have to ask him that."

Connie flinched, and felt an electric jolt jump along her nerves. "Wait," she said suddenly. "There are other paintings like this one, by the same artist?"

"That's right," the man nodded. "Two others."

And then he said no more.

2.

Connie burst through the front doors of the Hoyt Harbor grocery store and stood blinking owlishly in the sudden gloom. Heads turned towards her. She was breathing hard. A man wearing a long grey apron tied around his waist came towards her with a frown of concern.

"Can I help you, lady?"

Connie nodded her head, caught her breath. Her shoes were in her hands. She looked up into the man's worried face.

"I need to see Mr. Ryan," she said. Her heart was thumping in her chest and she could feel the throb of a twitching nerve at her temple. "Mr. Warren Ryan, please."

The man bobbed his head, then looked past Connie through the open door of the store as though maybe there was some kind of a crisis out on the street. It wouldn't be the first time two cars had collided or a child had been clipped and knocked down by the choke of tourist traffic. "Is everything okay? Are you okay?"

"I'm fine," Connie said, "but it's important I speak with Mr. Ryan personally. Is he here? My name is Connie Dixon. The people at the gallery on the waterfront sent me."

The man's face went through a myriad of puzzled, confused expressions like he was trying to piece this all together to make sense. Finally he seemed to give up. He shrugged his shoulders. "Wait here," he said, then turned on his heel and disappeared down an aisle full of tourists.

Connie slipped her feet back into her shoes and stood impatiently in the doorway for several minutes until a tall, stooped man came wading through the crowds of shoppers. He saw Connie and his face registered blank confusion. He hitched up his sagging pants with both his elbows and then wiped his palm on the front of his shirt.

"I'm Warren Ryan," the man said, extending his hand. "I understand you're in some kind of trouble?"

Connie gave the man a flicker of a smile and shook her head. "No trouble," she said. She pressed at her hair and straightened her shoulders like she was meeting an employer for an interview. "I just need a little of your time – and hopefully your help."

Warren Ryan was in his mid-fifties – old enough to appreciate a beautiful young woman, but not so old that he had given up flirting. He had thick wavy hair, going grey at the temples, and a wide friendly face. He held Connie's hand for a second longer than necessary and then gave her his most charming smile. "Follow me," he said. "We'll go to my office. Damsels in distress deserve a little privacy."

The building was old and long – stretching the full width of the block. Connie followed the man down an aisle of soda bottles and packaged snacks, and then up a concealed flight of steps to a small door. The grocery store was air-conditioned, but up here the air was warmer. Ryan unlocked his office door and stood aside. He gestured with an elegant flourish of his hand and Connie stepped into a little cubicle with a desk, a couple of chairs and a filing cabinet. It looked to Connie like the local police had gone through the office with a search warrant. There were piles of papers strewn across the desk and a tower of folders propped on the cushion of a chair. Over the desk was a small lamp, casting a bright pool of light onto a telephone and a small black iron box. Ryan muttered an apology and put the cash box in the top drawer of the filing cabinet, then scooped up the folders and set them on the floor. He gave the upholstered seat cushion a perfunctory brush with his hand and motioned for Connie to sit.

"It's tourist season," he said apologetically as if that explained the clutter.

Connie smiled and sat like a beautiful bird alighting. She swept the hem of her dress demurely down over her knees and clutched her handbag in her lap. Ryan dropped down into his chair with a weary sigh and then his expression became grave.

"Okay, you have my attention. Now, how can I help you?"

Connie hesitated for just a moment, searching for the right words, and then realized there were no right words. No matter how she phrased it in her head, she sounded on the edge of insanity.

"I understand from the people at the local gallery that you own two paintings that were made by a local man named Bill Mason. I would like to see them if I may."

Ryan made a curious face and sat back in his chair. He steepled his hands together and gazed thoughtfully at Connie past the tips of his fingers.

"What makes you think I have these paintings?"

"The gallery owners. They told me. I offered to buy the painting they own, but they refused. They said you had two other works by him."

"And you'd like to see them?"

"Yes."

"Why?"

Connie handed her card across the desk without a word. Ryan plucked the business card from her fingers and studied it carefully under the light of the lamp.

"New York?" he eyed her speculatively.

"That's right."

"You're a long way from home. Why are you here in Hoyt Harbor?" He didn't hand the card back. Instead he slipped it into the top drawer of his desk.

"I'm on vacation," Connie admitted, "and I'm also on the lookout for local artists worthy of representation by one of the most renowned galleries in the country."

"And you're interested in Bill's work?"

Connie nodded. "I liked the small painting the gallery had on display and offered to buy it. They said you might be willing to sell the pieces you own. I'd also like to meet Mr. Mason and talk to him about a career and possible exhibitions."

Warren Ryan leaned back in his chair and rocked in silent thought. His eyes were narrowed, his brow furrowed into a heavy frown. For long seconds there was only the sound of a squeaking chair spring. Connie watched the man carefully. The air in the cubicle was stifling. The man's shirt sleeves were rolled up to his elbows and there were sweat stains under his armpits. He gave a heavy sigh at last and swung his chair around until they were facing each other across the desk.

"I do have two paintings," Ryan admitted. "And..." he took a deep breath and paused on the threshold of decision. The winter had been lean for business, and no matter how strong the summer season was, he was already a long way behind with bank payments. "And, they are for sale," he said with reluctance. "If the price is right."

Connie felt a sudden leap of exhilaration and relief. She felt her heart slam in her chest and she had to fight the urge to bound from her chair. She choked back a gasp of breath and disguised it into a sound like clearing her throat. "I will need to see the paintings first," she said with restraint.

Ryan nodded. He rose to his feet and leaned over the bottom drawer of the filing cabinet. Connie found herself craning her neck with expectation, trying to catch a glimpse of the two new works. Ryan brought a cloth-wrapped bundle over to the desk and set it down. His expression was heavy with a reluctant remorse.

"I've had these paintings for five years," he said. He slumped back into the chair and left the bundle wrapped. "Ever since I met Bill and started taking care of his needs."

Connie tore her eyes from the tantalizing promise of the bundle. "His needs?"

Ryan nodded. "We make a delivery to his home each week – groceries," he shrugged. "Those kinds of things. Mr. Mason gave me these paintings the first time I delivered to his home. Their value to me is sentimental – you understand that?"

Connie nodded. "Doesn't he ever come into town?"

Ryan almost laughed. "Maybe once a year," he said. "Other than that he keeps private, keeps to himself. No one ever sees him and no one ever bothers him."

Connie couldn't help herself. Her curiosity was like an obsessive itch. "Is he... strange...?"

Ryan arched his eyebrows as though the question was a shock. He started to smile, but it wasn't an expression of amusement. Maybe irony, Connie guessed.

"No stranger than anyone else, I suppose," Ryan said after a moment of consideration. "I only met him the one time. Since then my son, Thad, has been making the regular weekly deliveries to the Mason property."

Connie asked nothing more and for a moment the room was silent. Connie felt her eyes once again drawn to the mystery of the wrapped bundle.

She trapped her bottom lip between her teeth and gestured. "May I see the paintings now?"

Ryan sat up straight and nodded apologetically. "Of course," he said. "I hope they are of interest to you."

He pushed himself out of the chair and stooped over the desk, adjusting the lamp so the bright pool of light fell upon the bundle. Then, slowly, as though the contents were priceless relics, he unwrapped the cloth so that Connie could see the first painting. Ryan stood back and Connie came slowly to her feet like a worshipper approaching a sacred altar.

Her face was white, the blood drained from under her tan, and her eyes were enormous pools of glittering wonder. Her mouth fell open and a little gasp of utter astonishment gushed from between her lips.

The first painting was another oil on an unframed canvas that had been drawn over heavy wooden stretcher bars. It was only ten inches square – a painting of two gulls on a barren beach, overshadowed by an outcrop of grey craggy rock.

It was stunning – rendered with such perfection that it seemed to transcend the canvas it was contained within and breathe its own life. Here was the magnificence of art, a painting so vividly made that it seemed to capture the wind and the sounds of the ebbing surf as though it had been crafted not with mere paint, but with some impossible dimension of nature's elements.

Connie felt her eyes glisten and blur. There was a sob of choked emotion in her throat. She touched her fingers to her cheek and was only vaguely aware that she was crying.

She pored over the painting, although she knew instantly the same hand made it, the same man. It was all there to see in his style, the effortless blending of color and the remarkable way the oil had seemed to melt into the canvas.

She looked up into Ryan's face. He was standing back from the desk, watching her from the shadows.

"It's beautiful," her voice husked with raw emotion. "Simply beautiful."

Ryan nodded. He had his hands clasped in front of him, his expression somber, as though he was somehow intruding on a private moment. Without a word, he carefully set the painting aside to reveal the second, larger painting.

Connie saw the seascape and clamped her hands over her mouth in speechless wonder. She blinked her eyes and realized she was visibly shaking. Slowly, she reached out tentative fingers and brushed them over the canvas, expecting them to come away wet, or perhaps covered in sand.

The second painting was another unframed oil on canvas, this one twice as long as the first. It was another seascape, similar to the one she had seen in the gallery. It depicted a lonely beach with a small boat drawn up on the sand. Beside the boat was the same beautiful young woman she had already seen, her back once again enigmatically to the artist, one hand extended as if reaching out towards the surly ocean that boiled in the mid-ground, slate grey beneath a thunderous sky.

"Are they good enough?" Ryan asked softly.

Connie nodded her head, not trusting her voice, not willing to sully this moment with any words. She gazed down at the two paintings and she knew instinctively that she had re-discovered greatness.

She snatched for the lamp and studied each painting minutely, examining the edges for signatures. There were none, yet still she was certain. She turned each canvas over with infinite care and saw no identification.

At last she nudged the light from the lamp aside and lifted her eyes to Warren Ryan. "How old is Mr. Mason?" she asked.

The storeowner shrugged. "Forty," I guess. "Maybe a little younger."

Connie nodded. It fit with what little she knew. A prickle of excitement tingled the hair at the nape of her neck.

"And you say he lives around here somewhere?" she kept her voice low, lest the excitement simmering in her blood became obvious.

"Sure," Ryan shrugged. "About an hour's drive out of town. He has a property on the beach."

"And you say he has lived there for the past five years?"

Ryan started to nod and then stopped himself. "We've been delivering groceries to him for the last five years," he said precisely. "I don't know about before then. I only moved here to take on this business seven years ago."

Connie fell back into her chair. She felt emotionally drained. There was a tremble in her thigh as though she had run a long way, and her arms had a heaviness that felt like the weary strain of exhaustion. She was numb with wonder, and yet overcome with the rare excitement of one who gazes upon lost treasure.

"I have a thousand dollars," Connie offered. She opened her purse and laid the money on the table. "Is that enough?"

Ryan narrowed his eyes shrewdly. He was stretched out on the financial rack, yet he sensed there was more to be made here. He had seen the woman's reactions to the paintings, seen the glittering need to have them in the way she lovingly gazed upon them. He shook his head and his expression became grim.

"Three thousand for both paintings," he countered. That would be enough to get the bank off his back and carry him through the next winter. "And it would have to be cash."

Connie looked down at the paintings on the desk and felt a surge of pure elation. They were hers. She would have them both.

She set her handbag down on the floor and pressed her knees together, straightened her back. "Mr. Ryan, can I borrow your phone?"

3.

Duncan Cartwright set his scotch carefully down and then casually reached between the pretty blonde's spread legs and teased her with the practiced touch of his fingers. The girl squirmed dutifully. Her eyes were wide, her head thrown back so that she stared at the ornate ceiling. Her jaw hung slack, and she was panting with feigned pleasure.

"Do you like that?" Duncan taunted the girl. She nodded her head, not trusting the betrayal in her voice. Her legs and arms were trembling from the strain of being propped on the antique desk, supporting her weight while the man amused himself.

She was young – no more than nineteen – with dirty blonde hair and a pretty face. She closed her eyes as he leaned forward to kiss her and she could taste the alcohol fumes and acrid stench of cigar smoke on his lips.

"I have great plans for your career," Duncan crooned. "It's all mapped out. First we'll exhibit you out of state – California perhaps... and then, maybe in another couple of years, we will do your first New York show right here in the gallery – if you're a good girl for me." He drew his hands possessively across her breasts. They were small, barely enough to fill his cupped palm, the nipples like perfect jewels of pink coral. The girl on the desk gave a soft moan.

Duncan watched the young woman's face carefully with a predatory fascination as his fingers played across her body in an arrogant attempt to arouse her, then he strode across to the chair where she had folded her clothes and snatched up her panties.

With the heavy drapes drawn, the wood-paneled office was almost dark, even though outside the New York skyline was bathed in the warm light of a sultry summer afternoon. The air in the room was a thick blue haze of smoke. Duncan came back to the desk and leered at the girl.

"Open your mouth," he said softly. "I don't want your screams of pleasure to disturb the gallery clients."

The girl opened her mouth with a wince of hesitation. Duncan pressed the silk of her panties between the girl's lips, then stood back and shrugged off his jacket.

The sudden sound of a phone ringing startled him. He scowled at the interruption and his mouth drew into a thin line of disapproval. He snatched the phone up and pressed it to his ear.

"I told you – no interruptions."

He listened for a moment and then a small frown formed deep lines at the bridge of his nose between the dark brooding eyes. He clamped a hand over the mouthpiece of the phone and turned on the naked girl. "Get your clothes and get out," he snapped. "Now."

The young woman scurried off the desk. He waited until she had fled from the room and then took a deep calming breath. "Put her through," he demanded.

He heard a click on the line and then a brief hiss of static. "This is Duncan, darling," he said urbanely.

"Thank God," Connie's voice down the long-distance connection sounded breathless with relief. "I wasn't sure you would be working today."

Duncan narrowed his eyes warily. "Wait a second," he said. "I'm putting you on speaker phone."

He stabbed buttons and then set the receiver down in the cradle. There was a brief crackle of sound and then Connie's voice again, amplified. "Can you hear me?"

"Yes," Duncan said. He lit a cigar and then clamped it between his teeth while he smoothed the fingers of both his hands through his hair. He saw the girl's panties. They had fallen on the floor at his feet. He picked them up, inhaled the musky scent of them, and then tucked the wisp of fabric into his coat pocket as a keepsake. "I was worried about you," Duncan went on smoothly. He stepped across the office to the window and raised his voice to cover the distance. "I messaged you several times last night. You didn't reply." There was an implied edge of menace in his words, even though his voice carried the tone of a concerned lover. He waited through a hesitation of guilty silence.

"My phone was stolen, Duncan," Connie lied. "I lost it last night. I stopped at a diner and my phone and handbag were taken."

"Where are you calling me from?"

"A shop in the town," Connie explained. "But I will replace my cell phone as soon as I leave here and message the number to you."

She waited through another moment of precarious, telling silence, and then asked softly, "Duncan, are you alone?"

"Yes. Why?"

"I need your help."

Duncan's mouth curled into a reptilian smile. "More money?"

"No."

"But wasn't your handbag stolen at the diner?"

Connie had to think quickly. "Yes... yes, it was – but it was stolen from my table while I went to pay for my meal. I have my wallet and money still."

More silence. Duncan drew back the drapes and a shaft of bright sunshine spilled into the office, casting light across the paintings of his private collection that adorned the walls. He blew a plume of smoke at the ceiling. "So what is it you want?"

"Advice – information."

"About...?"

Connie took a deep breath and held it for a moment. "About Blake McGrath."

Duncan's expression became a curious scowl. He strode back to the desk and fell into the big leather chair. "What exactly would you like to know?"

"Everything you can tell me."

"Can't you find this out on your laptop?"

"Yes, but it's back in the house where I am staying, and I need to know right now. Please..."

Duncan gave an amused, indulgent sigh. He sat back in the chair and the expensive leather creaked. He studied the glowing tip of his cigar for a moment.

"Blake McGrath is... or was... America's most famous contemporary artist," he began. "They called him America's Rembrandt. He won acclaim from gallery curators around the world and held special exhibitions at the Louvre and the National Gallery in London. Enough?"

"What happened to him?" Connie asked. "Why did he stop painting?"

Duncan drummed his fingers on the desktop. "Every exhibition the man held sold out," he said. "His last major showing was in New York about six or seven years ago. It was announced at the time that he was going away to create new works... but he was never heard of again."

"He just disappeared?"

"Off the face of the earth, so it seems," Duncan said. He had once owned a small McGrath seascape, and had hung it here in this very office as the pride of his collection, until a Saudi cartel had offered him a prince's ransom for the painting. As a reflex action, his eyes drifted across to the blank space that still remained on the wall.

"Can you remember the prices his work fetched – the ones from his last exhibition?"

"Of course," Duncan sounded almost offended. Art was his life, and more than the artists themselves, Duncan knew their values.

"He was the most renowned seascape artist in the world. His last exhibition contained twenty-four pieces. The largest sold for 1.6 million, and the smallest – a little study of some shells and rocks – fetched several hundred thousand."

There was a very long moment of silence, and Duncan thought perhaps the connection had been broken. His mind drifted back to the young girl he had sent from his office and he wondered if she still might be downstairs in the gallery... He plucked her panties from his pocket and ran the lace between his fingers.

Finally Connie's voice came back, lowered to a whisper. "If any new paintings of his were discovered, would they still fetch the same prices?"

Duncan paused and considered the question from an academic angle. The last Blake McGrath to come onto the open market had been a small seascape just twelve months earlier. It had been auctioned by Sotheby's for almost half a million pounds.

"More," he said with confidence, and then went on with a weary rush of impatience. "Connie, finding undiscovered works by America's Rembrandt would be like finding missing songs by The Beatles, or a new masterpiece by Picasso."

"Really?"

"Yes, really. Now, darling," he clenched his teeth as he muttered the endearment, "why are you asking me all these questions? I'm very busy here."

"I think I've found him," Connie said in a sudden gasp of breath. "I think I've found Blake McGrath."

Duncan straightened in his chair. In an instant the pretty girl had been forgotten. He dropped the panties, and his face became grave and stern as he leaned over the speaker of the phone.

"Explain," he barked the command.

Connie flinched, shocked by the sudden intensity of Duncan's voice. She gnawed at her lip and then went carefully through a veiled explanation.

"I'm in a little town on the coast of Maine..."

"You're not in Bar Harbor? You told me that would be where you are staying."

"No," she said. "I stopped overnight because I was tired," the deception did not come easily to Connie. She was, at heart, an honest woman, but there was so much at stake, and Duncan was not a man she owed her loyalty to. "I plan on driving the rest of the way up to Bar Harbor tomorrow morning."

"Go on," Duncan encouraged. He had a growing sense of unease and the cunning instincts of a fox. He knew he was being deceived. He could hear it in Connie's voice.

"Well I'm in this little town and I went to a local gallery here, just on a whim. Duncan, they have a painting by a man using the name Bill Mason – but I swear it's a genuine Blake McGrath. I think he's using the Mason name to hide. I think Blake McGrath is living somewhere here in Maine."

Duncan arched his eyebrows and his expression became incredulous. "And you're basing this assumption on a painting? Is it even signed?"

"No."

"Then what makes you think it's a genuine McGrath?"

"The style, Duncan! It's beautiful – utterly magnificent. And the name... Bill Mason, Blake McGrath. It all fits."

Duncan's expression soured. His impatience began to bubble over into the sharper tone of his voice.

"Do you have the painting?"

"No, but I have taken photos."

"Is there just one painting?"

Connie hesitated. "Yes."

"It's probably a forgery, or a coincidence. I mean every artist in the world has tried to paint like Blake McGrath. Isn't it more likely that you have just stumbled upon a talented amateur?"

Connie sighed. Her voice became very soft. "I suppose it is possible," she conceded, although she knew in her heart she was right. She knew with every fiber of her being that this was the work of America's master.

Duncan sat back in his chair and his voice became condescending, as though he were indulging a child. "Darling, you're not the first person to be fooled by a clever forgery, or to get caught up in a myth. The art world is famous for such deceptions." He paused for a moment. "Can I put you on hold, sweetheart? I have something important to take care of that simply can't wait?"

"Sure."

He clicked off the line and got through to his secretary. "That blonde girl who left here a few minutes ago," he growled. "I want her back. If she's not still in the gallery, go and look for her – and if you can't find her, start typing up your resume."

He took a deep breath and snatched up the line to Connie again. His voice changed in an instant, once again smooth and suave. "Maybe you've just stumbled upon another Han van Meegeren..." he offered reasonably.

Connie fell silent.

Van Meegeren was a Dutch artist during the 1930s who failed in his own career and then set about replicating the work of famous masters in the art world's most sensational case of fraud. So successful had the man been, that several of the world's foremost art critics had hailed one of his creations as the finest original painting by the 17th century master, Johannes Vermeer, that they had ever seen.

"Maybe..." Connie's voice stayed small.

Duncan sighed theatrically. "Look," he said. "Email me the photos and I'll take a look at them when I get a moment. And might I suggest you get yourself to Bar Harbor and watch some sunsets instead of chasing rainbows." He forced a smile into his voice, and then looked up suddenly to the sound of a reluctant knock on his door. The smile became genuine – and wolfish.

Duncan came out of his chair and leaned over the speaker. "Connie, I have to go," his words became clipped. "I'm sorry, darling, but I have an important meeting and I'm going to be busy for the rest of the afternoon." He hung up without waiting for her response and glided across the office. The blonde girl was waiting for him.

Connie hung up the phone and sat silently for a long time, Duncan's doubts echoing in her ears, and the two beautiful paintings on the desk compelling her eyes to them.

Logic said Duncan was right, but in Connie's heart she felt something more – some inner truth about these canvases. She made her decision.

When she came out of the office, Warren Ryan was waiting at the top of the steps. He looked at her hopefully. "What did you decide?" he asked.

"I'll buy them," Connie set her jaw. "Keep the thousand as a deposit. I'll bring back the rest of the money within the hour."

Ryan's face lit up in a smile of relief. Connie went out through the front door of the grocery store and stood, lost, on the sidewalk. She needed two thousand dollars, and she didn't have the money.

4.

The town had only one bank and Connie stood in line for almost twenty minutes as the harried tellers did their best to cope with the influx of demanding tourists. By the time Connie reached the plexiglass window, she had reconciled her decision and dealt with her guilt. She handed her cards across the counter.

"I'd like to withdraw two thousand dollars from this account," she smiled.

The young woman behind the glass thumped keys on her computer and then looked at Connie sharply.

"This is a joint account, right?"

"Yes," Connie said with a qualm in her voice. "My sister and I contribute money every week... and my employer makes additional deposits when required."

The cashier turned her attention to the computer screen for several moments, frowning. She set Connie's card down on the counter and spoke to another bank employee in quiet whispers. Both women came back to the counter and the older woman turned her attention to the display. She glanced at Connie.

"The bank has instructions to release a monthly payment from this account to a nursing home facility outside of Exeter," the woman said. "There have been no other withdrawals..."

Connie nodded her head. "Yes, that's right," she said. Connie and her older sister, Jean, had been struggling to both contribute to their mother's care since she had fallen at Jean's home three years ago. The money each daughter deposited was enough to cover the care facility's payments with little left over.

The older woman wrenched her mouth into a pout. "There is another monthly payment due to be withdrawn in a week," she explained in a veiled warning. "You should be aware that if there are insufficient funds in the account at that time, the bank will be forced to deduct charges. Do you understand that?"

"I do," Connie nodded her head. "I only need the money for a few days. There will be plenty in the account to meet the withdrawal when it is due, I assure you."

The woman shrugged. She nodded to the young teller, and Connie felt a giddy lift of relief as the money was handed across to her. She would have to phone Jean, but by then she prayed, it wouldn't matter.

5.

When Connie went back to the grocery store, Warren Ryan was waiting for her in his tiny office. Connie laid the money out on the table and the man counted it, stacking the cash into neat bundles with miser-like precision.

He slid the two paintings across the desk and Connie carefully re-wrapped them. "I also need directions to Mr. Mason's home," she reminded Ryan sweetly.

The grocery store owner nodded absently. The money, and what it meant for his business, distracted him. He glanced across at Connie and then reached for the phone. He thumbed a button and held the mouthpiece out like a microphone. "Thad Ryan, come to the office please. Thad Ryan." Connie heard the voice over speakers beyond the office door, the sound tinny and disconnected.

Ryan dropped the phone back into its cradle and scooped up the money. He locked it in the cash box and slid the filing cabinet closed just as there was a faint, respectful knock on the door.

"Come."

A young man stepped into the crowded space. He looked about twenty years old. He had a lantern jaw and blonde sandy hair, bleached platinum by sun and surf. He was broad shouldered, his skin the tanned color of toffee. The young man's face glistened with sweat.

"You wanted me?"

Ryan nodded. He clapped the young man on the shoulder and introduced him to Connie. "This is my

45

boy, Thad," he smiled fondly. "He makes the weekly deliveries to Mr. Mason."

Connie stood and shook the boy's hand.

"Miss Dixon needs to know how to find her way to the Mason home," Ryan explained dismissively. "I want you to answer any questions she has, okay?"

Thad nodded. Connie and Ryan shook hands goodbye. She tucked the precious package of paintings carefully under her arm and followed Thad down the stairs and out through a dark corridor to the store's loading dock at the rear of the building.

There was a large truck reversed up against an open roller door. Thad went down a nearby set of concrete stairs while two uniformed men with transport trolleys wheeled cardboard boxes off the vehicle and into the storage area. Connie followed the young man until they were standing under the shade of a tree. There was a cool breeze blowing off the ocean, and a scar of dark boiling cloud on the distant skyline.

"I'm not so sure Mr. Mason is going to welcome a visitor," Thad began with a warning.

Connie smiled. "That's okay," she said. "I was planning on phoning him first."

"You can't do that."

"Why?"

"No phone," Thad shook his head.

Connie raised an eyebrow. "Oh," she said, and after a moment she shrugged and smiled blithely. "Well, I'll just have to take my chances then."

Thad stared at her but said nothing for many seconds. Connie could see the glint of doubtful

46

speculation in his eyes. He bent and plucked at a long piece of grass and began tearing it into small shreds.

"How far down the coast does Mr. Mason live?"

"About an hour," Thad offered. "You follow the road out of town and head south until you see a turnoff onto Jellicat Road."

"Jellicat?" Connie repeated the unusual name.

Thad nodded. "Once you see that turnoff, you drive for another ten minutes until you come across an old mailbox. It's green. That's the track through the pine trees to where he lives."

Connie paid close attention. Her brow furrowed into little crinkles. "Once I find the turnoff – the one with the green mailbox – how far down the trail do I drive?"

"All the way to a gate," Thad said. "That's the start of his property. It runs right down to the coast."

Connie looked surprised. "The man lives on a beach?"

Thad nodded. "He owns some land. But his house is on a hill overlooking the beach. Suppose that's one of the reasons people around here call the place what they do."

Connie was paying close attention, giving every word importance. Suddenly she became intrigued and held up her hand for pause. "His house has a name?"

Thad smiled ruefully. "Nothing official," he explained. "It's just that all the locals call the place the light house."

Connie flinched. "Mr. Mason lives in a lighthouse?"

"No," Thad said. "We just call the place the light house because every light in the house is always on – night or day, it don't matter. Local fishermen say they can see the Mason house for miles out to sea... so we started calling it the light house."

Connie widened her eyes with curiosity. "Why does he always have his lights on?"

Thad shrugged. "No one knows."

Connie thought about that for a silent moment. She was intrigued by the deepening mystery that surrounded the man, and yet the unknown also made her cautious.

"Does Mr. Mason live alone, Thad?"

"Yes."

Connie nodded. "Your father told me you deliver his groceries every week. I wanted to know..." she hesitated for a second, unsure how to proceed politely. "I wanted to know... do you deliver any alcohol to Mr. Mason?" she fluttered her hands in a timid gesture to apologize for the effrontery.

Thad shook his head and smiled reassurance. "He ain't no drinker if that's what you're worried about. The last time I delivered anything like that was a few months ago. A single bottle of wine, that's all."

Connie felt herself shed a little sigh of relief.

Thad frowned. "Strangest thing in Mr. Mason's weekly delivery is the roses," he added as a sudden afterthought. He threw the desiccated shreds of the grass on the ground and thrust his hands deep into the pockets of his jeans. Over his shoulder he heard the big roller door being hauled down and then the truck began to slowly pull away from the delivery dock. One of the men in the truck gave Thad a wave and he smiled back as the heavy vehicle roared away in a belch of black exhaust smoke.

"Roses?"

"Seven," Thad flicked his eyes back to Connie and nodded. "Every week. A rose for every day."

Connie blinked. "For a man who lives alone?" Her face became a mask of bewilderment, yet there was something touchingly romantic about Thad's revelation that plucked at her heart. She gazed at the young man with wide yearning eyes. She needed to understand the meanings behind the many enigmas surrounding Bill Mason.

Thad simply shrugged his shoulders, as though the man was as great a mystery to him as he was to the rest of Hoyt Harbor's local residents.

"Do you ever talk to Mr. Mason when you deliver his groceries?"

Thad smiled. "Of course," he said.

"What kind of things do you talk about?"

Thad frowned and thought. "Just the usual stuff, I guess," he said with a dismissive shake of his head. "The weather, the beach, fishing... things like that." He was starting to feel uncomfortable by all the questions, and there was a mountain of work that needed doing in the store. He cast a distracted glance at the sky and saw it was getting late. There were dark storm clouds creeping like black menacing fingers over the horizon.

"What kind of a man is he?" Connie persisted.

Thad blinked like he didn't understand the question, or maybe he didn't quite know how to answer. "What do you mean?"

Connie wasn't quite sure herself. She fluttered her arms as if she were reaching for the words. "Well... is he loud, angry... is he rude to you?"

Thad shook his head. "He's just a normal guy," he assured Connie and then started to walk slowly back towards the store. "Just a man who likes his privacy."

6.

Connie returned to the vacation rental and carefully packed the precious paintings in her suitcase between the layers of clothes she had brought from New York. She cast a quick glance around the bedroom. Her laptop was on the bedside table. She hesitated for a moment, wondering whether to email the images of the paintings to Duncan, and reluctantly decided she should. It cost her fifteen minutes, so that by the time she carried her suitcase out to the car, the day was darkening into the long shadows of dusk.

Connie drove south, one eye on the clock, and the other on the road. The miles and time drifted by and her thoughts began to wander back across the unanswered questions that surrounded the paintings and the mysterious man who had made them.

In the back of her mind was the nagging doubt that Duncan might be right – the paintings could just be the work of a talented amateur – for Connie had never trusted her instincts like this before.

It was the first time in her life she had followed her heart – allowed her instincts and intuition to lead her into the unknown with nothing more than a faint hope and naïve faith that maybe – just maybe – the little paintings in the suitcase might be the solution to her freedom, and salvation from the obsessive clutches of Duncan.

As Connie drove on, the cloud front suddenly passed overhead and immediately she was plunged into an eerie twilight, fraught with boiling black clouds and a sudden wild shriek of wind that swayed the mighty pine trees along the verge of the road and littered the blacktop with a hail of debris.

Connie clutched at the wheel as the wind buffeted the car. The world turned black and brooding. She flicked on the headlights and saw small branches fall like rain through the searching reach of the beams. She eased her foot off the gas and peered ahead into the storm. The temperature dropped dramatically, and then the first drops of rain detonated against the windshield.

Connie drove on. The rain came in spatters – enough to make the road slick and shiny, driven horizontal against the car by the wind that howled through the trees. Connie saw headlights up ahead and then a car parked on the opposite side of the road. As she drew closer she recognized the shapes of two hooded men. They were leaning over a vehicle, scraping away the shattered shards of glass of the driver's-side window. Connie's tires bumped over a splintered tree branch that was strewn across the road and she wondered if it had caused the damage.

After more than an hour of anxious driving Connie saw a bent and dented sign loom out of the night. She peered hard through the windshield, slowed her speed to a crawl, and breathed a heavy sigh of relief when she read the word 'Jellicat'. It was the first turn off. She crept past, gradually built up speed again, and then – finally – the heavens opened and the world turned grey and blurred with a thunderous downpour of torrential rain.

Connie glanced anxiously at the digital clock on the car's dashboard. She had passed the turnoff ten minutes ago. She knew the green mailbox must be close. She dabbed the brakes, felt the car slide a little before it gripped. Connie's heart leaped fearfully into her throat, and then a tree branch suddenly fell from out of the darkness and crumpled against the trunk of the car. She shrieked in fear and clamped the steering wheel tight. She stamped on the brake pedal and the front end of the car dipped hard on its suspension. Connie felt herself thrown forward against the seatbelt as the car's speed bled away dramatically. She swung off the road and sat with the engine idling for a full minute while the rain drummed against the car until her nerves settled and her hands stopped trembling. It was now completely dark. There were no roadside lights – just an endless smothering darkness. At last she nudged the vehicle back onto the blacktop, and a few seconds later she saw a clearing in the tree line – a turnoff into the night.

She was shivering with relief. She bumped off the road and onto a narrow rutted track that turned left and right into the teeth of the storm. Rocky outcrops loomed up around her and she heard long grass and shrubs scrape against the side of the car. The headlights bounced and swayed and she felt herself thrown about in her seat until finally she came to an area where the trees seemed to become stunted and the howl of the wind rose to a maniacal flute.

Somehow over the roar of the storm, Connie thought she heard the far off growling boom of the ocean. She hunched over the steering wheel, went cautiously around a long curve in the track – and then the car slid out from underneath her and crashed nose first into a ditch.

The impact of the collision jarred her back and snapped her head forward. She felt the coppery, metallic tang of blood in her mouth. She dropped her hands from the wheel and tried to push herself back. She was trapped at an impossible angle, tilted forward and to the side, so that the restraint of the seatbelt was all that held her in the seat. Connie started to sob with pain and the after-effects of shock. The headlights threw crazy angled beams of light into the surrounding woods.

Connie unfastened the catch of the seat belt and fell across the car, tumbled against the passenger door. She felt a white-hot lance of agony shoot through her knee. She wept with the torture of it and then pounded her fists frantically against the door. It was jammed shut, wedged against the side of the ditch. Sobbing, Connie forced the window down and then clawed her way out through the narrow opening, her injured leg dragging useless behind her. She tumbled onto her back in the mud, stared up into the howling black face of the storm – and then passed out.

7.

Connie awoke to the horror of slobbering jaws and the stench of foul breath in her face. Something wet slithered across her cheek and her eyes fluttered open then grew nightmarishly wide. A beast with foaming froth at its jaws was hunched over her. She choked on a whimper, and then screamed.

For a moment nothing happened. She filled her lungs again and then suddenly saw the blinding glare of a flashlight beam flicker across her face.

From out of the darkness a man's voice carried on the night. "Connie?"

She blinked. The beast hung over her like a black avalanche of menace. She tried to scramble away, before the man came from the far side of the car and knelt in the mud next to her.

"Back off, Ned," the man said softly. The beast took two steps away from Connie and then sat. "Good dog."

The man played the flashlight across Connie's face and then flicked the beam down across her body. She was covered in mud, soaked through to the bone. The thin dress she wore clung to her like a second skin and she was shivering uncontrollably. The man put an arm around her shoulder. "Can you sit up?"

Connie nodded. The man eased her head out of the mud and propped her back against the side of the ditch. He flicked the beam once more down over her legs.

With a tender touch, he pressed his fingers lightly to her knee. The skin there was broken and he could see a large knot of swelling. Connie winced and clamped her teeth down on her lip to stifle a cry of agony.

"Not broken, I don't think," the man said. His voice was steady and even — a deep resonate sound filled with a quiet kind of confidence and calm assurance.

"How do you know my name?" Connie asked in a bewildered croak. She searched the darkness for the man's face but it was hidden behind the glare of the flashlight. Past his silhouette she could see a sky full of shredding clouds and a slice of bright yellow moon, low on the horizon. It was still raining, but she sensed the worst of the storm had passed.

"Because when we found you a couple of minutes ago you were unconscious and I didn't want to move you until you came to," the man explained easily. "I went through everything in your handbag looking for a phone. Why don't you have a phone?"

Connie nodded her head slowly and blinked. Her eyes were heavy and filled with muddy grit. She felt lethargic, overcome by a sudden drowsiness so that she slumped against the man. "I threw it away..." she said before her voice trailed off.

The man grunted. "Do you think you can walk?"

It took a monumental effort for Connie to open her eyes. She nodded her head. The man put his arms around her and lifted her. She came up onto her feet, and then her knee buckled. She staggered against the man and his hands wrapped around her. For a long moment she was pressed to his chest, could feel the muscled resilience of his body and

56

inhale the man smell of him. The unexpected intimate embrace was a shock, and her eyes flung themselves wide. She looked up into the man's darkened face but said nothing.

The man slung the strap of Connie's handbag over the big dog's head and then he lifted her in his arms and held her across his chest. She laced her fingers around his neck, felt the warmth and strength of the man's body radiate through his sodden shirt and she clung to him until the shivering subsided into tremors.

The man walked, carrying her away into the dark night, and to Connie, the gentle rhythmic sway of his steps was like being rocked to lulling sleep in his arms.

8.

When Connie next awoke, she was laying on a sofa, swathed in blankets. Her head was propped up on the armrest. She blinked, and her eyes adjusted to the light. She turned slowly and saw the man who had rescued her, standing by a stove in a neat kitchen. He was wearing clean dry clothes – a pair of jeans and a shirt with the sleeves rolled up his forearms. She watched him silently for long moments as he moved about, and then at last he seemed to sense her gaze upon him. He turned suddenly and came towards her, carrying a mug.

Connie heaved herself upright with a groan. The blankets slipped off her and she snatched at them to drape around her shoulders. She was cold and covered in aches. Her wet dress clung to her uncomfortably and her hands and arms were muddy. The man held out the mug and she wrapped her fingers around it gratefully, then inhaled the steaming aroma of coffee.

"Thank you," she muttered. The man propped himself on the edge of a chair in front of her and Connie looked up into the stranger's face.

"How long have I –?"

"Only an hour or so," the man smiled, and the gesture framed his mouth with etched lines like parentheses, and cast the hint of dimples high upon his cheeks. He had a strong jaw, shadowed gun-metal blue with stubble, and a mop of dark hair that curled about his ears and collar so that her first impression was that he had an almost boyish charm.

Then she saw his eyes, set within the sun-weathered face. They were dark – the eyes of a man who was accustomed to searching far horizons – clouded by a mysterious depth of concealed emotion that mesmerized her.

"How are you feeling?" the man asked.

Connie sipped at the coffee and felt the scald of it against the back of her throat. "Some bruises," she shrugged and fell silent for a heartbeat. "Thank you for rescuing me."

The man made a dismissive gesture. "It's Ned you should be thanking," he said. "He's the one who found you."

The man glanced across the room to where a giant Great Dane sat on a bed mattress. The dog was black, its head and body huge. It was watching Connie with brown soulful eyes.

Connie nodded and smiled across at the dog. "Thank you, Ned," she said softly and the dog thumped the end of its tail, recognizing the sound of its name.

She turned back to the man – felt her heart flutter when his gaze trapped her. "He's huge," she said.

The man nodded. "A gentle giant." He snapped his fingers and the Great Dane came off his bed and sat obediently beside the man. The dog's mouth fell open and Connie saw the pink tip of its tongue as the man scratched behind the animal's ears with a casual kind of affection. "I think he heard the sound of the crash," the man explained. "We were on the beach, and then suddenly he went bounding away into the woods. That was when I saw your headlights."

"You were on the beach? In the storm?"

The man shrugged and a shadow of something secret moved behind his eyes. "We always walk along the beach at sunset," he said, like the words were a stilted ending.

Connie sensed the man's change in mood with an intuitive feminine understanding, and there was a guilty rise of reproach in her expression. She lowered her gaze to the contents of the mug and took another sip. For a long time there was silence so that all she could hear was the persistent drumming of rain on the roof until the man seemed to shake off the pall of his melancholy. He clasped his hands together and studied Connie closely.

"Were you lost?"

She nodded. "Sort of," she admitted. "I came south from Hoyt Harbor. I was looking for a green mailbox, but I couldn't find it. This was the first turnoff from the road..."

The man sat back, narrowed his eyes. "A green mailbox?" he repeated warily. "The only person anywhere around here I know of with a mailbox like that is Bill Mason."

At the mention of the name, Connie's face lifted and their eyes met. Connie felt a little flutter – some giddy thrill – and she had to glance away before her attraction became transparent.

"That's right," she said with a rise in her voice. "That was who I had come to find. He's a local artist. He lives around here, somewhere."

The man nodded slowly. "I know him," he said, and then paused. "What makes him so important you were willing to almost get yourself killed driving through a storm to find him?"

Connie made an ingratiating face. "I'm from New York," Connie said, then took another sip of the coffee. She could feel the warmth of it spreading in her empty stomach. "I represent one of the country's finest and most prestigious art galleries. I saw some of Mr. Mason's breathtaking paintings in town, and I wanted to meet him."

The man sat back in the chair and his eyes became flinty. "Gallery," he said the word with the same kind of derision that other people would say 'lawyer'.

Connie winced. "You're not an art lover, I take it."

The man didn't answer. He got to his feet and went back to the kitchen, making a slow circuit of the little room, checking dials on the stove and re-arranging coffee cups, and then paused at a window and stared out into the black night.

Connie watched the man for several moments and then looked around her. It was a pleasant space that appeared to have been expanded in size some time in the past. She got the sense that the living room and kitchen were the heart of the home, but there were corridors and hallways branching out in several directions with closed doors that must lead to bedrooms. The floors were wooden boards, covered in rugs that had been thrown down without any real attempt at decoration. She glanced around the walls. There was a sagging old bookcase, groaning under the weight of paperback novels across the far side of the living room, and a large undraped window set beside the front door. There was nothing hanging on the walls, and no ornaments on shelves. Nothing that suggested the

61

house was a home – nothing to show that it was anything more than a building that served as shelter.

When the man came back into the living room at last, Connie could see the hardness had gone from his eyes. "You need a shower," he said. "And you will stay here tonight."

Connie's face registered shock and a flicker of alarm. "No, I can't do that," she said, and got to her feet instinctively. The blankets fell from her shoulders so that she stood before him in only the damp little dress that clung to every curve of her body. She became aware of the fact that she felt almost naked and exposed with a sudden blush of self-conscious panic. "I couldn't..." her knee buckled and she winced as needles of pain shot up through her thigh, all the way to her hip. She threw a desperate hand out for the armrest of the sofa to steady herself and there were fresh tears of agony in her eyes.

The man arched his eyebrows in a challenge and he smiled without any trace of humor. "The shower is down the hall," he said in a no-nonsense voice and pointed past Connie's shoulder. "I'll help you."

He hooked his arm around her back and she let her weight fall against him like a crutch. She could feel the press of his hip against hers and the tender strength in his grip. She hobbled down a passage until the man stopped before a closed door. "I'll find you something to wear," he said. "Take your time. There's plenty of hot water. When you're done, I'll wrap your knee. You should be right by the morning."

She nodded and then caught her breath. "My car!"

The man's mouth pressed into a thin line. "I have a truck. I'll tow you out tomorrow. The car didn't look too banged up. I think you'll be fine to be on your way."

Connie shook her head. "No, I have a suitcase on the back seat. It has clothes... and some personal things..."

The man frowned for a moment and then took a breath. "I'll go and fetch it," he said.

She smiled her gratitude. The man pushed open the bathroom door and Connie used the doorframe to support herself. She teetered on the threshold for a moment while the man reached behind him into a linen press and then ducked under her arm to set fresh towels on the bathroom vanity and start the shower running. A billow of steam swirled across the floor. The vanity mirror was already fogged and the bathroom carried the lingering warmth of recent use.

"Are you going to be able to undress yourself?" the man asked with only genuine concern in his face. Connie jerked her head in a nod. She felt somehow gangling and skittish being so close to this man and she was sure she was blushing. Despite her pain, she could feel a burning flood of hectic color on her cheeks as he fixed her with his steady gaze.

"Yes," she said. "Thank you. I will be fine."

The man started to close the door behind him and then stopped suddenly. He stared down at the floor for a moment of decision and then raised dark, troubled eyes to Connie.

"Are you good at your job?" he asked softly.

Connie was taken by surprise. She considered the question objectively. There were just a few inches of space between them, the man's closeness and the tone of his voice somehow intimate.

"Yes," she said. She held the man's gaze.

He nodded. "And so you know art and artists well?"

Connie nodded. Said nothing.

The man shut his eyes and sighed, like a haunting burden from the past had come upon him. "Then you know that Bill Mason is really Blake McGrath, right?"

Connie trapped her lips between her teeth, her body racked with a strain of tension. "Yes," she whispered. "I know."

The man nodded again. He looked away, seemed to choke on words that were like broken shards of glass.

"I'm Blake McGrath," he said at last.

Before Connie could react – before even the realization could show on her face – he drew the door quietly closed behind him and left Connie alone with her shock.

9.

Blake stood on the front porch and stared out into the dark night. The wind off the ocean had an icy chill, and he could hear the percussive boom of the surf as the lingering tail of the storm carried through the swells. He draped a heavy coat over his shoulders and glanced back through the open door to the living room. Ned was lying on his bed, but he was alert and watching, waiting for Blake to beckon him. Blake held up the palm of his hand and the dog set its great head down between its paws in disappointment.

It was still raining, sweeping across the coastline in isolated downpours so that one moment the sound on the old iron roof was like the thunder of a thousand drums, and the very next moment there was almost eerie silence.

Blake turned the flashlight on and went down the steps, splashed through the mud, following the track back to Connie's stranded car.

He went into the dark with the anger upon him.

Deep down, he had always known that this day would come – must come – for the art world was one of ancient heroes and immense riches. It would never quite forget him, never let him become just a memory. But he had not anticipated this. He had not expected to be discovered after all these years by a young woman. He had always believed the moment would somehow be tainted with the tarnish of greed when they found him, not the apparent wonder of one woman for his craft.

Somehow the notion seemed so pure that it was naïve.

For seven years he had lived on this rugged, isolated piece of coastline, and the first two years had been the happiest of his life. He had worked, invigorated and inspired by the majesty of the sea and her many faces, her many moods. He knew that time of his life had been the pinnacle of his career. Each new painting that came off his easel had been better than the last, each new canvas was a fresh wonder of infinite skill and passion so that there was a point where even he himself was almost content.

Almost – for no true artist can ever be satisfied or ever feel they had captured the perfection and majesty of nature. But he had come close; near enough to at last grudgingly accept the admiration of others and not feel like a fraud for the clumsiness of his devotion.

Yet none of those paintings had ever been shown, for the ocean that had inspired him and driven him to the heights of his career had turned on him – taken that which was so precious as to be priceless. The ocean had robbed him of life, of love, until all that he wanted was to hide, turn his back on all that had been, and wash away his misery in hopeless tears of heartbreak.

He had coveted the loneliness, drowned his sorrow in a mire of misery so that it left him emotionally scarred in a way that would never leave his life.

And in the despondency of those dark days, so too had gone his passion, his gift, until he had thrown down the brushes in despair and vowed never to paint again.

Five years of a life sentence of guilt had been served on this barren beach, this broken rocky coast. And now the world had found him. It was as though the ocean that had dragged him down into a deep dark trough had suddenly determined to wash him stranded and unwilling onto the shore again.

The irony was that it was all too late...

When Blake reached the car his blood was pounding at his temples. He slipped in the mud, crashed against the driver's side door, then flung it open and climbed across the chaos. He forced the passenger window up to shut out the rain, switched off the headlights, and then twisted at the waist to reach across the back seat. The suitcase had wedged into the foot well. Blake heaved it free, then hauled it back out through the open door. He gave the door a nudge and the tilted angle of the crashed car worked with gravity to slam it shut.

A squall of grey slanting rain swept across the path and Blake ran heedless through it. The wind came through the trees in undulating moans, a debris of dead leaves fell from the sky. He clutched the suitcase against his chest and forced himself back into the darkness until at last he saw the bright lights of the house and he slowed to a stagger, and then a trudging walk.

The futile anger that had come upon him had gone – been burned away to become despondency. He went heavily up the porch steps and stood shaking the rain from the coat. He could hear the hiss of water in the plumbing. He draped the wet coat over the porch bannister and carried the suitcase through the front door. Ned raised his head with a look of curiosity but Blake didn't notice the dog. He went through to the bedroom at the end of the corridor and set the suitcase on a floor rug.

He heard the shower water cut off at last and he tapped lightly on the bathroom door.

"I got your things," Blake called out. "They're in my bedroom, down at the end of the hall."

To his surprise, the door cracked open an inch and Connie's face peeked through the gap. Her face glowed with freshly scrubbed color and her hair was wet. She smelled of soap. Drops of water clung to her lashes. She was leaning around the protection of the door so that her face was all he could see, and he realized with a shock that she was pretty.

"Thank you," she said.

Blake flicked his eyes away, stared at a space an inch above her head with a twinge like guilt. "Do you feel better?"

She nodded. "Much."

There didn't seem to be any more to say. Blake shuffled his feet, found something interesting on the floor to focus his attention on for an awkward moment, then simply turned and walked away towards the living room.

10.

Connie came hobbling from the bedroom wearing a dress that hung to her knees and a mismatched sweater against the coolness of the night. Her hair was wet, combed out so that it hung black and shimmering down her back. She wore no makeup and Blake saw that her lips were the pale pink color of coral, her face squarish so that her features created a vulnerable and tender kind of beauty. He watched her sag onto the sofa, her injured leg still painful enough that she grimaced, before he sat down carefully beside her.

He ran his hand lightly across her knee, felt the swelling, and then rested her leg across his lap. The skin was abraded, but most of the damage was obviously internal. He wrapped the injury gently with a pressure bandage so that her leg was stiff and unmoving.

He set her leg down and then asked her to stand.

"I'm not a doctor," he said. "This might just help to support your weight and allow you to drive to medical attention. With luck the swelling will go down overnight."

Connie got to her feet and took a couple of rigid steps with her jaw clamped. The pain was less – a dull throbbing ache. She eased herself back onto the sofa and thanked him with her eyes and smile.

She was sitting disconcertingly close to him, Blake could feel their thighs touching and the press of her through the stuff of her dress and the denim of his jeans seemed to burn like fire. He was unnerved. He leaped to his feet and went to the kitchen, called over his shoulder to her as he went.

"How do you like your coffee?"

"Just like before, thanks," Connie said. There was a reedy waver in her voice, for she too had felt the same tremors of heat from the innocent contact.

When Blake came back, he was carrying two mugs. He handed one to Connie and then chose the seat across from her to sit. He sipped at the coffee, watching Connie's face over the rim of the mug.

"Why are you here?" he asked at last.

Connie set down her mug. She clasped her hands in her lap and seemed to lean forward as she spoke, as if to give her words greater sincerity.

"I found a small painting in a Hoyt Harbor gallery," she began softly, holding his gaze, her eyes never wavering from Blake's. "And when I saw it... I wept, because it was one of the most beautiful paintings I had ever seen in my life."

She sat back, took a deep breath, and then went on to explain how she had purchased the two paintings from Warren Ryan and realized that the name Bill Mason was a veil for Blake McGrath.

Blake listened, his features seemed to be carved in granite. He was unmoving, watching Connie's face, her eyes, and her expression with wariness.

When she had finished retelling her story, Connie lapsed into empty silence. Her lips were parted, glossy and soft. "I fell in love with your art," Connie added in a whisper, "and I wanted to know if my heart was right – if my instincts could be trusted. I wanted to find out who the man behind the work was, and what drove you to create the most beautiful paintings the modern world has seen... and why you suddenly disappeared."

Blake raised an eyebrow. The woman seemed sincere, yet he had learned to be miserly with his trust. The fact was that she had come from a gallery, and every commercial gallery survived by making a profit.

"How much did you pay for the paintings?" he asked.

"Three thousand dollars," Connie said softly.

Blake smiled wryly. He remembered the works. He had given them to the grocery store owner. "Well I imagine you will be able to turn a tidy income," he said in understatement. "Together, they're worth probably half a million, maybe even a little more."

Connie nodded, but then her eyes widened and she began to slowly shake her head. "They're not for me," she explained. "And I didn't buy them to gain from directly."

He was surprised, but he tried to conceal it. "You said that you were good at your job," he challenged her.

"I am," Connie said earnestly, "But I am a lover of art, not a lover of money, Mr. McGrath."

Blake winced. Coming from this woman the formality of a name he hadn't heard uttered in five years sounded too impersonal, too distant.

"I called you Connie, back at the car," he said tactfully. "Please call me Blake."

She smiled then, and her whole face seemed to light with a sparkling glow of unaffected beauty. Blake felt something tight squeeze in his chest and it took an effort for him to raise his wary guard again. Sometimes, he reminded himself, nature's most beautiful creatures can be her most dangerous.

"So now you have found me," he said and lowered his chin onto his chest gravely. There was a moment of heavy silence in the room. He tried to smile but his lips would not hold the shape. "So what more do you want?"

For a moment Connie's face was blank with innocence. "I would love to see any other paintings you have made," she admitted shyly... "and I would like to ask you why?"

"Why what?"

"Why you disappeared. Why you have never exhibited again."

Blake stared hard at Connie. There was shadowy movement behind her eyes and he could not tell if it was deceit or sincerity, for her voice and body language betrayed nothing that he could match to her expression.

"I don't paint any more," he said.

Connie looked appalled. Her expression became stricken with shock. She felt something squeeze painfully inside her. She could accept that this man had hidden his work, accept that he chose no longer to share his gift with the world, but to stop painting seemed too tragic, too cruel.

"Why?" the word escaped her in a scandalized breath.

Blake shrugged, but said nothing. His expression darkened as though he could deflect the needle of the question with an inscrutable scowl. He stared into his coffee mug for a long time and then gave her a sideways glance. She looked pale, and he instinctively knew at last that she was genuine. He sighed. He could see a private pain like hurt in her solemn enigmatic eyes and he suddenly wanted to make that look go away — to offer something gracious that might retrieve the situation.

"I'll show you some paintings," he compromised. "Works that I did when I first moved here, seven years ago. But I won't answer the personal questions," his voice took on an edge of warning. "Can you accept that?"

Connie nodded, but kept her expression veiled. Someone had hurt this man, she realized intuitively. At some time in the past, someone... or something... had left Blake McGrath broken, and altered the course of his life.

11.

Connie followed Blake down a long passageway that ran past the kitchen, and then into a large cluttered room at the far end of the house.

His art studio.

Connie stood in the doorway, her eyes taking in everything in an instant. In front of a large window on the opposite side of the room she saw his easel, a high triangular frame that stood at least six feet tall. In front of the easel was a backless chair on casters, and beside the chair was a small kind of bookcase, perhaps a couple of feet high and wide. The bookcase was on the same kind of casters as the chair. The shelves of the box were crammed with tubes of paint and rags, and atop the box was an old-fashioned wooden palette and several paintbrushes. Everything was layered in a thick coat of grey dust.

"I don't come in here any more," Blake seemed to sense the direction of Connie's eyes, and offered the explanation. Connie nodded, said nothing. She took several steps into the room, and her eyes swept from the ceiling to the floor.

"It's color-corrected light," Blake explained the complex grid of tracks and globes that hung in clusters overhead. "I had a team of consultants and electricians create the system, so that the light in the room would be natural and constant. That's why it looks like daylight in here – even in the middle of the night. The globes don't give off the typical yellow hue that could affect the colors while I was working."

Connie nodded again. She still had not spoken. Her eyes went to the furthest wall from where she was standing and settled on a timber rack of high vertical shelves. Stored upright, like library books, were over three-dozen canvases, each one wrapped within cloth, each a different size and shape.

Connie went towards the rack in a kind of reverent trance. She carefully caressed the edges of each bundle, needing to touch them, as if she could pick up some other sensory vibration of the marvels they might contain. She turned back to Blake who was watching her from the doorway. Ned was standing by his side, tongue lolling from his slack jaws.

"How many paintings do you have stored here?" she asked in a softened awe.

"Thirty one," Blake said. "What you are looking at is everything I created for an exhibition."

"The one you canceled?"

"Yes."

She frowned. "But, you had the paintings."

"Yes. But that's not the reason I canceled the show, and it's not the reason I stopped exhibiting and painting."

He came into the room, Ned at his side like a silent shadow. The big dog found a piece of rug-covered floor in a corner and dropped to the ground with a weary sigh.

Blake went to the easel, turned it so that it faced into the room, and ran the palm of his hand over the frame to wipe away the dust. Then he slid the first canvas from the vast timber storage rack, and set it on the crossbar of the easel, still covered by its dust cloth.

"You need to stand back near the door," he said to Connie.

Connie took several steps away. Blake stood beside the painting and took hold of one corner of the cloth.

"Remember," he said, "these are over five years old. You might not like them – they might not live up to your expectations…"

Connie gave him a murderous glare of impatience and urged him to reveal the canvas. Suddenly the world seemed quiet to her. The sounds of the rain and wind seemed to fade, for all her attention was focused on the easel and what it held.

Blake sighed, and then drew away the dust cover.

Connie felt herself go cold with an unnatural chill. She took a step towards the painting, and then stopped herself. She stood, trembling, her eyes huge and dark in the paleness of her face, her lips parted as though the moment was somehow breathtaking and sensual.

The canvas was a couple of feet wide and perhaps eighteen inches high – not a large piece by modern standards, and yet the work seemed to explode at her in a clamor of surging sensations. It was a Blake McGrath seascape, painted with the master's unique touch of drama and pathos.

The painting showed a rugged stretch of distant coastline, greyed and blurred by a sullen sky, yet in the midst of the clouds was a shaft of golden light, breaking through the overcast and spilling its color onto the sandy foreground. On the beach was the tragic figure of an elderly man, his head bowed, standing amidst the broken ruins of an old boat while the ice green swells of an angry ocean burst upon mid-distant rocks in explosions of white spray. There was something haunting about the work, and in the way the man and boat had been rendered, so that Connie felt inexplicably saddened. She covered her mouth with her hand and stared at Blake with a gaze of bewildered awe.

"How do you do that?" she whispered hoarsely. "How do you capture such powerful emotion on canvas?"

Blake frowned, bemused. He leaned over the painting and glanced at it. He remembered the work, recalled the difficulty depicting the shaft of sunlight. He had been pleased with the finished painting, but now Connie's profound reaction forced him to take another look at the work. Technically it was good.

"It's just a painting," he said.

She looked appalled. She shook her head. "No," she said dramatically. "It's not. It's a gift, Blake. It's something in the way you work the paint, some part of *you* that's infused into the image. It's as if you can create intense emotion through paint."

Blake felt a rush of relieved delight. For some reason he didn't understand, this woman's approval of his art was important to him.

Connie came to the easel and bent close to the painting, her eyes alight, her expression rapt as she gasped at the intricate little details that combined to give the work dimension. Blake watched her with secret pleasure. Her hair was drying and he could see delicate little whorls around her ear, like fine and silky breaths of perfection. He inhaled the fresh scent of her and was mesmerized by the interlace of her long lashes when she blinked. He had the sudden reckless urge to reach out and caress the flawless skin of her cheek with the tips of his fingers, and the insane shock of it made his senses tilt.

Connie turned her head then, looked deep into his eyes for a solemn moment that seemed to stretch like the soulful caress of a lover's fingers, until at last Blake flinched and glanced away.

"Do you want to see more?" he asked brusquely, his voice too loud in his own ears. He strode across to the storage rack and fetched one of the bigger paintings. His fingers were trembling.

Connie hooded her eyes but there was an enigmatic Mona Lisa smile on her lips. She nodded her head without speaking.

Blake scooped up the first seascape, wrapped it with perfunctory tosses of his hands, and set it on the studio floor. He stood the new canvas on the crossbar of the easel and at last cast his eyes back to where Connie waited.

"This one is called *'Daybreak',*" he said. "It was my favorite piece. I was going to make it the feature painting for the exhibition, and use the image for the gallery catalogue and marketing launch," he explained. "It's the closest I ever came to being satisfied with one of my own works."

He took a step back and unveiled the painting with a little flourish.

Connie felt a rush of blood flush across her cheeks and her heart slammed hard against her chest.

The painting was three feet wide and two feet high, a view from a high cliff top that depicted a panoramic scene of the ocean in all its furious majesty. Under a pale dawn sky, shot through with the colors of sunrise, was a heaving swell exploding upon craggy sentinels of rock. The moment had been captured when the wave was sweeping towards the shore, the green boiling surf just beginning to curl and break.

"It's a masterpiece," Connie breathed. She felt overwhelmed. There was vibrancy in the colors and a hulking energy in the wave that was utterly stunning.

Blake shook his head. "There is no such thing as a masterpiece any more," he said, and Connie flashed him a withering glare, as though, surely, there was no painting quite so perfect as this.

"That's just a hackneyed term people use," Blake went on. "It has no relevance nor significance." He tossed the dust cloth down on the chair and went to stand beside Connie, staring back at the painting as he spoke.

She felt the casual brush of his shoulder against hers and she did not move away. "I think you're being very humble," she said softly, as though she was gazing at some revered religious artifact.

"No, I'm serious," he said, and turned to look at her. "Masterpieces were exactly what paintings once were," he explained. "They were works of art painted by a master. Back in the sixteenth and seventeen centuries, in particular, an artist was a qualified tradesman, just like builders are now, for example. Artists served an apprenticeship of several years during which they actually learned every facet of the craft, from canvas preparation to mixing paint. At the end of their time they were masters. A painting made by a master was a master piece." He saw in Connie's eyes that she was listening with fascination, though he suspected this was something she would already have known. "These days, anyone can paint – anyone can buy brushes and a canvas and then sell their work. There are no great masters anymore, and with their demise went the right to claim any modern painting as a master piece."

Blake fell silent. Connie turned her eyes back to the beautiful painting. Beside this man, she felt like she was standing in the protective shelter of some great stone pillar. At last the temptation of the art became too much. She crept quietly towards the easel and began to pour over the intricate way the wave and white cascades of water had been replicated.

"Your brushwork intrigues me," Connie said when she was only inches away from the painting. "Most artists who work in oils are always so thick with the paint, as though they use it to help create textures and dimensions. Even a lot of the great past masters did that," she turned and glanced over her shoulder. "But in your paintings, it's like the paint just melts into the canvas. It's very unique."

Blake twisted the corner of his mouth into a little smile, as though this was a comment he had heard about his work countless times in the past. "I guess I could have done the same kind of thing," he admitted. "Like most painters, I was certainly influenced by the old masters... but I suppose I just have a different way of working. It's not something I ever really set out to do. What you see in that painting is just a style thing."

From somewhere else in the house a clock chimed several times. It was a dull sound, muted through closed doors. Ned suddenly raised his head, the dog's expression a sad eyed question. Blake nodded, and the Great Dane lifted himself slowly to his feet on arthritic legs and crept quietly from the room.

Connie turned from the canvas and smiled up into Blake's face curiously. "Where is he going?"

"The beach."

"Why?"

"Because he goes down to the beach every night at this time," Blake said. His voice had become hollow, and his brow had corrugated into a deep frown.

"Why?"

"To sit," there was a strain creeping into his tone like a warning.

"For how long?" Connie softened her voice and tried to take the edge off her question.

"Until sunrise."

Connie wanted to know more, but Blake's eyes had become flinty and there was a rigid defiant set to his shoulders.

"How old is Ned?" she asked instead.

"Six," he said.

Connie sensed she had brushed against a part of Blake's life that was still like a tender wound, raw and painful. She had stirred memories and regrets within him and she wished vainly for some way to retrieve the intimacy – to be able to turn time back to when they had been discussing his art. It seemed suddenly that the small distance between them had become an icy crevasse.

"Do you want me to go?" she asked timidly. She rose then, facing him across the space.

"No," he said. His mouth was drawn into a thin pale line, and Connie could sense some inner struggle behind his eyes.

"Can you tell me about your technique?" she offered. "Did you paint from photographs?"

It was an olive branch extended; an invitation for him to rejoin her and reach across the void. Blake nodded his head stiffly, and began to speak again. At first his words were stilted, his posture still reserved, but gradually the color came back into his voice and Connie silently rejoiced in the passion that rose from within him as they talked deep into the night.

"I used photographs for reference," Blake showed her a drawer of images that had been the foundation of some of his best-known earlier paintings. "Nature is too fluid – a beautiful woman with an ever changing countenance – so that to try to capture an instant of her glory is impossible for a plein air painter," he said. "So I would take photographs, and from those I would choose the moment I thought she was at her most glorious, or her most terrifying. Then I would paint live."

"Why was that necessary?" Connie led him on, intrigued, and felt him opening up to her once more. "Couldn't you have stayed in your studio and merely re-created the photograph?"

Blake nodded. "Yes," he admitted. "But I didn't ever want to capture the two dimensional image of a photo. I wanted to capture the *elements*. For me it was important to paint on site." He laughed suddenly and it was an irresistible sound that sent a delicious shiver down Connie's spine. "The photos gave me the moment, but being out there," he cast his arm towards the darkened window, "being on the beach, helped me to appreciate the awe and grandeur."

"So your paintings became a kind of composite?"

Blake arched an eyebrow, a little disconcerted by how readily Connie had seemed to understand so perfectly. He had spent hours explaining his methods to others who had never been able to grasp the abstract of the concept.

"Yes," he said and found himself gazing into her eyes through a long searching moment of tingling silence, his dark eyes burning like fire at her soul. "That's exactly what they were – a composite of what the camera saw and what the elements stirred in my heart."

He drew more paintings from the racks, each one a dazzling jewel until Connie felt as if a vast treasure surrounded her. Blake pointed out the problems with each of the works, the areas that had caused him frustration and had forced him to re-evaluate his techniques until at last Connie's leg throbbed painfully and her face became drawn and pale.

Outside, the darkness of the night was absolute. The moon had slid across to the sky's far horizon and taken with it the wind and the rain so that there was only stillness above the lulling rumble of surf on a distant shore.

"Blake," she laid a gentle hand on his arm and the touch of her fingers sent an electric shock through his spine. It was the first time she had deliberately touched him, and they were both silently aware of the moment. "You can't keep these paintings hidden from the world," she implored him. "They deserve to be shown, not kept here, wrapped and concealed. They're too beautiful – too magnificent. To hide them like this is... it's a tragedy."

Blake's cynicism was instinctive. "Shown, or sold?" the question was like a challenge, a test.

Connie shook her head. "Show them – sell them if you want," she said earnestly, "but at least let the world see them."

Blake let out the breath he had been holding and felt a rush of relief. She was not like the others. This was not a conceited play for a gallery commission.

He said nothing. Connie was still staring up into his face. "The work you have here must be worth ten or fifteen million," Connie whispered, awed by the realization of her own words.

"I have all the money I need," he said.

"Then show them – put them on display and let people enjoy what you have made. Blake, paintings are like books, they need an audience to come alive. Let the world be enchanted by these stories, and experience the emotions. Don't let them die unseen. Don't let their fate be this," she swept her arm wide in a gesture that encompassed the dusty studio, as if it were an ancient tomb.

Blake felt himself instinctively leaning towards her, but he stopped at the last moment. Connie had sensed his movement and swayed towards him in anticipation, her body becoming tense with a craving for his touch. Blake reeled back on his heels and his gaze became clouded.

"I'll think about it," he muttered vacantly. He took a step back and turned away to wrap one of the paintings in its cloth.

Connie made a little pout with her lips to show she was disappointed, but not surprised. Then she looked on for silent seconds and gave herself over to the pleasure of quietly watching him. His body was lean and toned, the muscles in his forearms well defined, and the ones in his shoulder and across his chest rippling under the cotton of his shirt. His skin was polished and browned by a thousand suns. It was a man's body – one that had been honed by long hours outdoors and manual work. Yet his hands were the hands of a surgeon, the skin smooth, and the fingers long and tapered. He was a contrast – a man comfortable in the harshness of nature, yet with an exquisite deftness of touch and a creative flair that was genius.

She thought then about Duncan, and the vast differences between them. Duncan had the frame of a dancer, narrow hipped, but with the flesh beneath his expensive clothes turning soft and pallid from the excesses of his life. He was immaculately groomed, urbane and sophisticated, yet ultimately false and shallow. The façade he presented hid a dark and dangerous devil behind the mask of a handsome face whose features had begun to blur at the edges with plump pouches of indulgence.

Connie blinked. She had been staring at Blake, but seeing that other man. Now her attention came snapping back and the hint of a smile brushed across her lips. Blake had finished wrapping the painting. She watched him carry it across to the storage rack and slide it onto one of the narrow shelves.

Connie had never known a man like this; he had her admiration and respect. It was not only the legend that surrounded his rise to the pinnacle of the art world, or the years he had passionately devoted to his craft. It was his presence – the calmness, the sureness that radiated through his demeanor, and yet also, she conceded, there was the feminine attraction for the broken man – the one who had suffered in some tragic way that she wished she could heal. He seemed unaffected with the temperament and precocious arrogance that tarnished so many of the truly gifted, yet utterly shattered by some circumstance that had altered the course of his life.

She was captivated.

Connie came alert suddenly. Blake was watching her from across the studio with a curious expression on his face.

"Sorry..?" she stammered.

"I asked if you were smiling, or grimacing," he repeated.

She blushed. "Smiling... and grimacing," she fluttered her hands like little birds. "I was just thinking how much I have enjoyed tonight – listening to you, and feeling very privileged to have seen your paintings. But, I must admit, my knee..."

"Of course. I'm sorry." Blake suddenly seemed to become aware of the lateness of the hour. The time had passed as if he had been in a trance. "I'll help you back down the hall. You can sleep in my bed tonight. I will take the sofa."

"Oh, no," Connie looked genuinely aghast. "I couldn't – "

"You have to," he smiled into her eyes and she felt herself catch her breath. "Because I insist."

12.

When Connie woke the next morning she sat up in the bed with a start. She had the sense that it was late. She could hear the boom of surf on a beach, and the hiss of waves running up across sand. There was a cool breath of breeze, pillowing the net curtain that hung across the bedroom window. She slid her feet off the bed and found to her relief that she could stand without much pain.

She changed into a t-shirt and faded jeans, then limped along the hall to the living room. The house seemed empty.

She went out through the screen door and onto the old porch. The colors of sunrise had long ago been smudged into a perfect blue sky. Connie shielded her eyes from the glare of the sun with her hand and stared down past a hedge of low stunted bushes to a crescent of lonely beach between rocky outcrops, like craggy stone watchtowers.

The beach was just a few hundred yards long – a narrow strip of white sand shaped into a gentle coastline curve. The rocks to the south rose up from the ocean as part of a pine tree covered headland, and in the far distance, hazed along a blurred horizon line, she could see other promontories that marked the southward coast of Maine.

The breeze across the ocean diced the indigo depths into a million glittering shards of sunlight and ruffled the tops from the waves. They rolled towards the shore lumpen and round-shouldered and then spilled upon the sand so that it shone wet and glistening like gold.

There was a wandering trail of footprints along the beach, and at the end of the trail stood Blake and Ned, the lonely silhouettes of man and his loyal dog near the northern headland, where the rocks jutted out into the surf like an ancient break wall. Blake was standing very still, staring out across the endless ocean. Ned was close at his side. The spent foaming wash of the waves lapped around their feet and left behind little twists of seaweed amongst the seashells along the tideline.

Connie leaned on the porch rail and inhaled the smells of salt and surf, letting the warmth of the sun wash over her. She lifted her face to the sky and closed her eyes as though to be kissed by a lover, and felt her soul drenched with the simple joy of being alive.

At last she went down the porch steps, the breeze tugging at the tendrils of her hair and flattening her t-shirt against her body. Little swirls of sand kicked up at her feet. She walked towards the low hedge of shrubs, and then suddenly, from the corner of her eye, she saw her car, parked away from the house in the shadow of an old flatbed truck.

Connie widened her eyes in surprise. She turned towards the car. The front passenger side of the hood was a little dented, and the wheels were crusted in mud. She circled the vehicle, saw another indentation and scratches on the trunk. She opened the driver's side door and leaned inside. The upholstery was wet, the interior smelled like drying clothes.

"How did you sleep?"

She turned with a small start. Blake was standing at the corner of the house. He was wearing blue jeans, rolled up to his knees and a simple white shirt, the top buttons undone. He folded his arms across his chest and Connie saw crisp little whorls of hair curl from within the deep V of the shirt.

"Wonderfully, thank you," Connie straightened and swept the hair from her face. "And thank you for salvaging my car," she smiled helplessly. "When did you do that?"

Blake shrugged. "Earlier this morning," he said as though it was no trouble. "She seems fine. I took her for a quick drive back down to the main road. So long as you don't hit high speed, you should make it back to town in one piece – although you should have a mechanic check the tires and the wheels for balance."

Connie nodded guiltily. "I can't thank you enough for rescuing me last night," she said shyly. "I'm very grateful..."

Blake held up his hand. "Don't mention it," he said. "I enjoyed having you here – enjoyed your company."

They stood in silence for a moment. Connie felt her face flushing with awkward color. She smiled brightly and Blake smiled back.

"Before I go," she began at last, "could I ask you one last favor?"

Blake nodded. He shuffled his feet in the gravel driveway as though he was bracing himself.

"The two paintings I bought from Warren Ryan..."

"Yes."

"They're unsigned."

The corner of Blake's mouth twitched into the hint of a knowing smile. "And...?"

"Would you sign them for me?"

Blake fixed Connie with steely eyes. "You realize if I sign those paintings, it will double their value?"

"Yes."

"Is that why you bought them? Is that the real reason you came here? To somehow compound your investment?" The words as he spoke them sounded callous, yet he had to know. He wanted to believe this woman had been genuine.

Connie shook her head. "No," she said and her eyes became wide with a hint of hurt. "I told you last night – I am an art lover, not a lover of money. And those paintings are not for me. One will be sold to pay for my mother's nursing home care. The other will..." her voice tailed off guiltily.

"Will what?"

Connie sighed. She felt a lump rise in her throat and a sting of tears at the corners of her eyes. "I'm in trouble," she said in a rush. "The second painting will clear my debts, give me a fresh start."

Blake watched her eyes, studied her face. Her embarrassment and hurt were genuine. He relented with a breath of relief.

"Then I will sign them for you," he said.

13.

He carried the two paintings into the studio and cleared a space on a wide counter-top. He laid the paintings out and went to his easel to fetch paint and a fine brush. Connie stood back, not wanting to intrude. Blake hunched over the first canvas and pushed his face close. He squinted his eyes. After a moment he signed the bottom corner of the painting with his trademark flourish and then turned his attention to the larger painting.

"If I sign these in oil, they'll take a week or more to dry," he said over his shoulder. "So I've done the signatures in acrylic, okay?"

Connie nodded. She had her hands clasped in front of her hips and she was gnawing on her lip.

Blake turned back to the counter-top. He flipped each painting over, mindful of the drying signatures, and wrote an inscription in pencil across the back of each painting. Connie watched, holding her breath. She saw Blake blink in a curious myopic gesture, and then rub at his eyes with his knuckles.

He waved Connie closer and stood back from the counter.

"I've personalized a message to *'my good friend Connie'*. That should help the value a little, but the dates are from when I made the paintings. Do you understand why?"

Connie didn't. She looked up into his eyes with unfeigned innocence.

"You're to tell no one where I am, Connie. No one. You are to let me maintain my privacy. If I date these inscriptions for today, people will know you have found me, and I want to be left alone. Do you understand?"

Connie nodded. "I swear," she said in a grateful gush, "that I won't tell anyone where you are, Blake. You have my word."

14.

They stood on the driveway, just a few feet separating them. Connie's suitcase with the precious paintings was on the back seat. The driver's door was open, and the engine idling in soft little burbles of sound. She had her purse in her hand. She offered Blake one of her business cards.

"In case you ever get a phone..." she said with a smile.

Blake glanced at the card and tucked it inside his shirt pocket. "You will be the first person I call," he promised.

Ned came loping down the porch stairs to join them, his big head hanging between his shoulders, and he padded to where Connie stood and leaned against her.

"He wants a pat," Blake said. "He knows you're going, and I get the feeling he's not too happy about it."

Connie scratched behind the Great Dane's ears affectionately. The dog closed its eyes and stretched its hind legs. His weight was enormous and Connie found herself giggling suddenly. She ran her hand down the dog's back and his jaws hung slack. Then, quite suddenly, the big dog snatched Connie's purse from out of her fingers and went scampering away towards the beach.

Blake looked on in stunned disbelief for a split second. Connie let out a little yelp. They stared at each other – and then went chasing down the sand in pursuit of the Great Dane.

Ned dashed out of sight at a scurrying run, his long powerful legs carrying him across the dry sand and down to the tideline, the vibrations of his massive weight through the ground as heavy as the drumming hoof beats of a horse. He hit the wet sand, turned with an excited wag of his tail, and then trotted off towards the southern end of the beach, Connie's purse still clutched lightly in his mouth, his head held high with a prancing pride.

Connie and Blake ran after him. Blake's footing went from under him and he rolled, then bounced back up to his feet. Beside him Connie was laughing. Blake dusted himself off, glared after the big dog, and then started to run again. Suddenly he was laughing too, and the sound was such a shock to him that it sounded foreign in his own ears. He pounded across the dry sand, then hit the hard wet sand at last, feeling the strain in his calves ease.

Connie had sprinted ahead and Blake watched her with covert delight as he chased doggedly; her legs were long and finely shaped, the jaunty roll of her bottom and hips a delicious provocation as they swayed with each stride. She was splashing through the white foaming wash, her hair streaming out behind her. Blake heard the high tinkle of her laughter and realized he was grinning broadly.

At the end of the beach, Ned stood waiting. His tail beat against the air and his big chest heaved. He saw Connie slow and then approach with giggling stealth. Ned's eyes were alight with mischief. He took two steps towards the waves and Connie shrieked. She made a lunge for him. Ned jinked one way, the weight coming onto his

95

shoulders so that he hunched like a compressed spring, and then he ducked beneath the embrace of Connie's arm and went trotting triumphantly back up the beach. Connie turned, knee deep in the surf – and then a wave swept in from behind her and burst against the back of her legs.

She squealed with the ice-cold shock of it, held her arms wide as the wave washed around her. The water sprayed up her back and she stood like a sodden scarecrow for long seconds, her mouth agape, gasping.

Blake stopped running... slowed to a dignified walk. He went towards the edge of the surf and could not conceal his mirth.

"Oh," Connie's voice became a sweet threat. "You think this is funny, mister?"

Blake put his hands on his hips. He was breathing deep but steadily. With the sun behind her, Connie looked like some beautiful vision that had risen from out of the watery depths.

She began to wade in towards the beach, her eyes fixed on Blake. Behind them Ned came down from the dry sand and gently set the purse at Blake's feet, then trotted off again towards where two seagulls were bickering.

"Do you think this is funny?" Connie asked again. Her voice had become silky smooth and made menacing by the wicked gleam in her eyes. She flashed Blake a dazzling smile, and then bent and splashed him with water.

Blake flinched, then gasped. The water was a freezing shock. Connie laughed, and then saw Blake lunge at her. She wailed with delicious fright and went splashing away from him, lifting her legs in high steps above the surging water.

At last she came from the surf, gasping and shivering with the cold. She eyed Blake warily, waggled a finger to warn him from retribution, and then sat down, still laughing, still panting.

She saw Blake's shadow loom over her. He was holding her purse. He dropped into the sand and they stared out at the ocean, laughs dwindling to happy smiles and finally a sigh of exhaustion and contentment.

Blake watched the horizon line for long minutes, feeling the warmth of Connie's body brush against his. He glanced at her furtively. Connie had her eyes closed, and there were sparkling droplets of water hanging from her lashes.

She was beautiful, he decided.

He saw Connie's eyes flicker open and his gaze darted guiltily back to the skyline. The gulls that had drawn Ned's attention suddenly took to startled flight. They skimmed the surface of the waves and then went wheeling and dipping away across the ocean.

Blake heard Ned panting, and then the pad of his big paws on the sand. He glanced quickly over his shoulder – and caught Connie gazing at him with a captivated expression on her face.

She made a pretense of blinking sand from her eyes to conceal her fluster, but even to her own ears her voice sounded unnaturally breathless.

"Your dog is the devil," she said

"He's never done anything like that before," Blake shook his head. "Maybe he doesn't want you to go…"

Silence.

Blake could hear his own heart thumping, hear Connie's steady breath. The words seemed to linger between them and he groped for something to say to salvage the moment.

"Your jeans are wet," he said quickly. "You should take them off."

Connie turned to him, her face a sudden pantomime of incredulous lady-like horror, but her eyes sparkling with glee. "I beg your pardon?" she rasped.

Blake looked baffled for a moment until he played the words back in his head. Then the blood drained away from his face and became white with dread. "Oh, God," he said in alarm. "No! I didn't mean that!"

Connie laughed and laid a casual, reassuring hand on his arm. Blake felt the skin beneath her touch catch fire. "It's okay," she grinned, and held the smile on her lips as they stared into each other's eyes. Her expression became solemn. In an instant, the chasm between companionship and intimacy seemed to shrink to almost nothing. It would take just one small step...

Blake saw something move behind Connie's gaze, some liquid stir of secret emotion. She parted her lips and the entire world seemed to go quite still. Blake clenched his jaw and leaned away from her, breaking the spell.

"It's getting cool," he said, his words hollow. His heart was beating as though it might break out of his chest. "And you should give yourself plenty of time to make Hoyt Harbor before nightfall."

He got to his feet and she stood beside him, said nothing. They trudged back up the sand towards the house, the chasm between them widening again with every step.

15.

It was another hour before Connie was once again ready to leave. She had changed clothes, pulled her hair back in a ponytail. She stood on the driveway gangling and awkward as a teenage girl. Ned watched on, chastened and banished, from the porch.

Blake reached deep into his pocket and held out a bundle of cash. Connie frowned.

"When I went through your handbag looking for your phone, I noticed you had no money," he said. "This is five-hundred dollars. It should be enough to get you home – or wherever you are going."

Connie started to shake her head. "Blake... I can't," she said. "I can't take money from you. You've done so much for me already."

Blake shrugged. "Connie, it's only money. If you won't accept it as a gift, then consider it a loan. But either way, you're not driving away from here without money for emergencies."

Connie sighed. She was fighting back tears of gratitude. He had known that she was in trouble, yet he had offered this money without condition. She took the cash reluctantly, then her expression became fierce. "A loan only," she promised. "As soon as I can I'm going to repay you."

Blake shook his head. "It's not –"

"Yes," Connie insisted.

She carefully tucked the money into her purse and then looked past him, down to the lonely beach and the rolling crests that foamed white against the sand.

"I'm going to miss this place," she said to Blake on a sudden impulse of emotion. "It's a piece of paradise."

Blake's face remained impassive. "Not for me," he said enigmatically. "I hate it."

Connie looked shocked. She stared up into his eyes as though maybe he had been joking, but what she saw there left her flinching and troubled.

"You mean it," she gasped.

Blake nodded his head. "I mean it. It might have been paradise once, but now..." he shrugged his shoulders with sadness. "It feels like a prison."

She searched his eyes again, saw the change in his expression and knew enough about the man now not to ask more. A gull flew in from the beach and circled the house. Connie watched it for a moment.

"I wanted to be a famous artist," she confided softly. "I wanted it so bad. I wanted to have the big exhibitions, hear the adulation of the critics... but I never had your talent," her voice was small and shy again. "So I changed dreams. Now I want my own gallery – a place for great art. Nothing pretentious," she flashed him an impish grin. "Just something I can be proud of."

Blake inclined his head. "It sounds like a nice dream," he said. "And if that's what you want, then you should chase it, and never let anyone stand in your way. But be careful," he raised a finger in sudden caution. "Sometimes the dreams we set for ourselves can turn into nightmares. Be careful what you wish for."

Connie listened, watched Blake's face, the way his mouth moved, the way the corners of his eyes crinkled when he turned and looked towards the sun – the minute facial expressions that were like gusts of wind or clouds that preceded a change in the weather.

"It sounds like you're speaking from experience," she prompted him gently.

Blake nodded, stared down at the ground for an instant, then looked back into her eyes. There was darkness in his face.

"My dream was always to paint," he said softly, and his voice sounded suddenly far away, like a whispered echo. "I wanted to be the best – to make the kind of paintings that would touch people emotionally – turn art into an experience," he said.

"And you did," Connie said loyally.

The look in Blake's eyes sharpened suddenly. "But when I got there – when I was finally at the top of my mountain, Connie, I realized too late that I had forsaken all the things that mattered in order to climb to the peak of my career."

He looked into Connie's eyes. "Don't make my mistake," he implored her with a desperate passion she hadn't heard in his voice before now. "Don't take your focus off what matters in life. Remember to never forget those you love or care for – don't let fate make you regret your choices."

Connie nodded solemnly, and then threw her arms around his neck. She kissed him chastely on the lips, felt the hardness of his chest press against her breasts. "Thank you," she whispered. "Thank you for everything."

She turned then and slid in behind the wheel of the car. Her cheeks were on fire, her hands trembling fiercely. Without daring to meet his eyes again, she turned the car around and went away down the driveway, her heart racing and her eyes just a little misted.

Blake stood in the silence until long after the car had disappeared. He touched his fingers gently to his lips. They were still moist from the kiss. He glanced at Ned, and the big dog pricked back his ears and looked up, puzzled.

"She was nice," Blake said.

Ned yawned, then settled himself to the ground and propped his head between his paws, like he was waiting for her to return.

16.

Connie left the car with a mechanic on the outskirts of Hoyt Harbor and walked down to the foreshore. The afternoon had turned cool. The breeze across the harbor abraded the surface into dark ripples so that the boats nudged and bumped restlessly at their moorings, and the umbrellas over the café tables fluttered like war banners.

The wind chased away the crowds of tourists, and the market stallholders along the promenade packed away their wares with one eye on the darkening clouds that scudded across the sky.

Connie went to the end of the wide pier and stared away through the harbor entrance to where the surf was crashing against the break wall, and a thin mist blurred the sky and the sea into a smudged line without definition.

She could live here, she decided suddenly – she could grow accustomed to the laid back lifestyle of coastal Maine. She thought about her tiny apartment in New York, the thronging crowds that filled the city and the constant jar of noise that she had grown accustomed to. The city had an undeniable vibrancy that was like an energy, which swept people up and carried them along. In contrast, even the summer crowds here along the coast were no comparison, and she found herself idly wondering what towns like Hoyt Harbor would be like in the winter. She imagined deserted streets, local store holders hunkering down to wait out the long cold months until the tourists returned. Then she thought about the dream she had confided to

Blake – her dream of a gallery. Hoyt Harbor – or any other sleepy town along the coast – could never compare to the mighty commercial influence of New York City. But did that matter?

Connie didn't think so. Surely, she reasoned, if the art she stocked was of good quality, then the tourists would come from the cities – and the internet had made dealing in quality art a global business. Maybe, just maybe, a little gallery somewhere on the coast of Maine wouldn't be the worst way to make a modest living.

The thought made her smile. She drifted back along the pier, and wandered into a café that was just beginning to fill with early dinner guests. It was still daylight – the setting sun was hidden somewhere behind a scar of grey cloud. Connie found a table in a corner with a view of the harbor through the full-length glass windows, and she sat down with a weary sigh. Her knee ached a little. A waitress brought her a menu and Connie asked for change, then went to the pay phone in the corner and first phoned the mechanic.

The car was repaired, and the damage had been largely superficial. The mechanic had left the car beside his workshop garage and the keys were waiting in the mailbox in front of the building.

Connie thanked the man and hung up. She hesitated for a moment, took a deep, grim breath and set her jaw. Then she phoned her sister's home in New Hampshire.

It was an awkward call. Jean's voice sounded concerned, and Connie was reluctant to say too much on the phone. She needed to see Jean face-to-face to explain what she had done, and she needed

Jean to see the paintings so she would be convinced. Connie put a carefree smile into her voice.

"I'm heading back early tomorrow morning," she said. "I thought I would stop by the nursing home and visit mom, then spend tomorrow night at your house, if you don't mind a freeloader for a night. There are some things we need to discuss..."

Jean's voice came down the line with unfeigned concern. "Your boyfriend has called here twice looking for you," her sister muttered, the tone of her voice almost loathing.

"He's not my boyfriend," Connie denied.

"Okay, your boss. Duncan said you had lost your cell phone. He thought you might have contacted me. He seemed disturbed."

Connie nodded. "It's one of the things I want to talk to you about," she said.

"Are you all right? Are you in trouble?"

"No," Connie smiled. "Not any more – but the full story will have to wait until I see you. I should be there by this time tomorrow afternoon."

She hung up with a sigh of relief. The conversations between her and Jean had always been strained. Jean was nineteen years older than Connie, and since their mother had needed the care of full time nursing, the relationship between the sisters had become more like a parent and daughter. Jean meant well, Connie knew, but the two women had inherited different personalities and values from their parents. Jean was the steady one – the daughter who studied hard, worked diligently, and ultimately built an obscure life of moderate happiness. Connie had always been the indulged child – the daughter born at a time when her mother and father were the age of grandparents.

Connie went back to the table, ate a quick meal and then walked back across the bridge to the mechanic's. By the time she reached the repair shop her leg was throbbing and the last of the day's light had gone. She drove back to the vacation rental with her headlights on, and flung herself down on the big mattress with a weary groan of exhaustion.

There were four emails on her laptop from Duncan. Connie's fingers hovered over the keyboard, teasing herself – testing her resolve. Finally, with something that felt like an uplifting gesture of deliverance, she slammed the computer screen shut and left the messages unread.

Connie went to bed early. She was tired, emotionally drained. Her mind drifted to the the long drive south in the morning and then – sometime between sleep and wakefulness – she thought about the one thing she had promised herself not to dwell on. She thought about Blake McGrath.

His smile haunted her dreams.

17.

The nursing home was a low sprawling structure under leafy trees, just a few miles outside of Exeter. Connie parked the car and stood for a moment in the shade. The facility was set on rolling green grounds with manicured gardens and an idyllic duck pond nestled amongst long rushes. Connie's feet crunched across the gravel as she walked towards the sliding glass entry doors.

In the air-conditioned foyer she glanced around. She was overcome by the pervading sense that the home was a half-way house between a hospital and a funeral parlor. Despite the modern furnishings, the bright prints on the walls, and the profusion of flowers in vases, there was an air of lingering desperation that seemed to seep from the walls.

She smiled brightly at a woman behind a high reception counter, and introduced herself. The woman looked up sharply.

"Yes, we've been expecting you," the words were like a warning. "Your sister called to let us know you would be visiting today. Before you go through to your mother's room, would you mind taking a seat? The Director would like to have a word with you, I'm afraid."

Connie felt a rising sense of alarm. She clutched her hand to her throat and her eyes became fearful. "Is mom... is she all right?"

The receptionist nodded her head. "She's healthy," was all she would say. Then she picked up her phone and buzzed through to an inner office.

She spoke briefly, hung up the phone, and then gave Connie a little frown of annoyance.

"Follow me, please," the woman said crisply. She was in her forties, wearing a nursing uniform with a watch pinned on a chain to her pocket. "The Director will see you right away."

Connie was led through a warren of narrow passages and into a small office with spartan furnishings. A woman in her fifties or sixties with a care-weary face greeted her coolly. The woman was wearing a severe grey skirt and blouse. Her hair was scraped away from her bland face and tied back in a bun. She shook Connie's hand and invited her to sit with the ominous tone of bad news to come.

Connie sat with her back straight, her knees pressed together and her handbag clasped on her lap, leaning forward attentively. The Director went behind her desk and stood beside the chair as if she was more comfortable with the barrier between them.

"I wanted to discuss your mother," the Director said.

"Is she ill?"

"No," the Director shook her head. "No. She's annoyingly spritely, in fact. That's what I wanted to discuss with you."

Connie's brow furrowed into a frown of deep confusion. "I don't understand..."

The Director took a deep breath, held it for a very long time and then sighed. She had a pen in her hand. She tossed it down on the desk, folded her arms across her chest, and fixed Connie with a grey steely glare.

"Yesterday your mother pinched one of the male nurses on the bottom," the Director said. "The week before, she was found with a can of beer in her room – although heaven knows how she smuggled it in... and just last month she attacked our cat."

"Your cat?"

The director nodded. "Mr. Snuggles is a cat that has been adopted by the facility. He roams around the grounds and gives the residents comfort and companionship. He is also instinctive. When residents are close to passing, Mr. Snuggles seems to sense their time is near, and he sleeps at the foot of their bed. Invariably, the next morning, the resident has passed. It's as though the cat curls up to be of comfort..."

"And my mother?"

"She attacked Mr. Snuggles with her walking stick," the Director accused. "Frightened the life out of the poor little thing and chased him down the hallway. Now he won't go anywhere near her."

Connie sat back, felt the relief like a great weight from her shoulders, and suppressed a smile. "I am sorry," she said, her eyes sparkling. "I will talk to my mother about her behavior."

The Director nodded. "Please," she insisted.

Connie got to her feet. Her cheeks were flushed. "Is there anything else?"

"Yes," the Director puzzled. "A question. Was your mother actually one of Marlon Brando's lovers?"

"What?" Connie almost spat the question in incredulous shock.

"She told several of the other residents here that she was the lover of Marlon Brando."

110

Connie giggled. Her lips did all kinds of things to stop herself from laughing. She shook her head. "That's not true," she said. "My mother and father were married for over forty years before he passed away."

The Director nodded with a sour expression like she wasn't the least bit surprised.

"Can I see her now?" Connie asked sweetly.

The Director nodded. "I'll have one of the staff show you the way. I believe she is out in the garden. She apparently told one of the other residents that she was planning to steal one of the golf buggies we use to transport our most frail clients down to the duck pond."

Connie arched her eyebrows, and hid another grin behind her hand. She went back out into the foyer, and the receptionist who had greeted her on arrival led her down a wide passage with numbered doors on either side. At a T-intersection, the nurse turned left and Connie could see a sun-drenched garden area with lawn chairs nestled between the arms of the building.

"She's over there," the nurse pointed. Then she called out suddenly, her voice clear in the sleepy silence. "Ruthy! Your daughter is here to see you. Make sure you behave…"

A frail old lady, hunched down on a bench turned her head, the puzzled expression on her face clearing when she saw Connie standing in the shade. She waved to her daughter delightedly, and then flipped the receptionist the bird, thrusting the gnarled middle finger of her hand high into the air.

Ruth Dixon was a frail-looking old lady with withered arthritic hands, and a face lined by the creases of a long life beneath a shock of soft grey hair. She was tiny, the flesh withering on her bones, but her eyes were bright and glittering behind the steel frames of her glasses. She looked up into Connie's face with an expression of pure joy and lifted her arms. Connie bent over the bench, hugged her mother and kissed her on the cheek, her fingers feeling the feeble frame beneath the long-sleeve dress and the cardigan around the old woman's stooped shoulders.

"Hello, mom," Connie smiled warmly. "I hear you're still causing trouble for the staff. I've just been hauled into the Director's office about your most recent antics."

Ruth grinned with wicked mischief. Connie sat close beside her mother and the old lady clasped her hand.

"Hello, lovey!" Ruth's voice was a thin and reedy chirp. She studied Connie's face closely as if to remember every detail of her daughter. "Don't mind what they say," she lowered her voice to a whisper and leaned in conspiratorially. "The screws just want to keep me down."

Connie nodded and then turned away, amused. An elderly man shuffled across the lawn, supporting himself with a walker. There was a young uniformed woman at his side, holding the man's elbow.

Connie felt her mother's fingers squeeze her hand and she turned back. Ruth had a proud, contented smile on her lips.

"Are they treating you well, mom? Do you like being here?"

Ruth nodded. "I'm surrounded by old people," she lamented seriously, and flung a thin arm in the air to gesture her impatience, "but a couple of the screws are good. They look after me."

Connie shook her head in mock horror, and tried to admonish the old lady. "Mom, they're not screws, they're nurses. This isn't a prison." She paused for a thoughtful second. "Would you prefer to live with Jean again?"

Selling one of the paintings she had would make that possible, Connie realized. Her mother could move back to Jean's home and be with family. The house could be renovated to accommodate her. There might even be enough for regular visits from nursing staff to the home.

"Oh, hell no!" Ruth's face became wide-eyed and animated with horror. "Lovey, if I hadn't fallen down those stairs at Jean's place I probably would have thrown myself down them. She's my daughter, and I love her... but the woman has absolutely no sense of humor!"

Connie couldn't help herself. She giggled and shook her head. "Well then stop giving the nurses such a hard time. The Director told me about the young man yesterday ... and the poor little cat."

Ruth gave her a scornful look. "That damned cat," she hissed. "I'll kick its ass if I ever catch it."

They lapsed into a contented silence. The sun was warm, and there was just a whisper of cool breeze through the trees. Connie sighed, felt weary muscles beginning to relax from the long drive back from Maine.

Ruth watched her daughter's face with a kind of knowing that only a mother could have. She waited until the elderly man and his nurse were out of earshot.

"Are you still on with that Dunstan?" she asked at last.

"Duncan."

Ruth shrugged like it didn't matter. "Dunstan, Duncan... whatever you call him, he's no good for you, lovey."

Connie turned, her expression curious. "How can you say that, mom?" she asked softly. "You've never met him..."

Ruth smiled, but it was a bitter touch at her lips without any trace of humor. "A mother knows," she said sagely. "A mother always knows. I don't need to meet the man. I can tell what he is like because how he treats you is reflected in your eyes and your face. It's all there to see."

Connie fell silent. She watched a workman on his knees, digging at a garden bed with a small hand-held shovel, grateful for the small moment of distraction.

"It's over with Duncan," Connie said at last. She was surprised how easy it was to say the words, how they spilled from between her lips with no regret – nothing but a bitter taste of resentment.

It was over with Duncan, she knew that, and it gave her a little lift. But it wasn't something she wanted to discuss with her mother. She hadn't come to share her problems.

They talked for an hour; desultory conversation with no purpose other than the closeness of companionship. Finally Connie got to her feet and glanced up at the afternoon sun. "Mom, I need to go," she said softly. "I told Jean I would stay with

114

her tonight, and then I'm driving back to New York tomorrow."

Her mother nodded, understanding, yet unable to hide the shift of sadness behind her eyes. "Of course, lovey," she patted Connie's hand. "Try not to fight with your sister. Remember, she doesn't have a sense of humor." The old woman winked, then sat back on the bench. It was getting cool.

Connie hesitated in the shadows of the doorway and watched her mother for a long moment, conflicted with a child's guilt. Then she set her shoulders and strode away down the long passage. She needed to be at Jean's place before nightfall.

18.

Her sister answered the door on the third knock. Connie stood on the front steps harried and weary. The drive had taken forty minutes through heavy traffic, including a stop at a thrift shop where she bought an old briefcase to carry the paintings. Jean answered the door with a wan smile, glanced down at the briefcase in one of Connie's hands and the suitcase in the other, but said nothing. She held the door open and Connie stepped inside the old house that was filled with the aromas of cooking and coffee.

The kitchen was bathed in the last of the afternoon's light, spilling through a window above the sink. Overhead cupboards had been replaced, and the stove was new, Connie noticed, but that was where Jean's money – or her will – had run out. The curtains across the window were pale and faded, and the kitchen counter was chipped old wood. Jean went to the sink and filled the kettle with water. Connie could hear the thump and knock of old pipes in the walls.

Jean set two enamel mugs on the counter, arranged sugar and a jar of instant coffee near her elbow, then turned back to Connie with a flicker of a smile while she waited for the water to boil.

"How is mom?"

Connie nodded. "She's good," she nodded her head sincerely. "Still getting into trouble, but she seems fine."

Jean made a tired face. She nodded. "The coffee shouldn't be long," she said in a brittle show of domesticity. "How was your drive back from Maine?"

"Good."

The superficial smile stayed fixed on Jean's lips. She began to say something else, and then seemed suddenly to remember her manners. There was a wooden table in one corner of the room. She waved Connie to a chair with a flutter of her hand.

"Please..."

The table was the kind of piece that interior decorators would call 'distressed'. There were dark marks and scratches in the surface, and ancient notches along the edges. Connie scraped back a chair and sat. She set the suitcase down beside her and laid the briefcase flat on the table.

Her sister reminded Connie of a dried flower, or maybe a black and white photo. Somewhere in her past, the color had been drained from her life, and Connie couldn't quite recall when. They had never been close – the age gap had prohibited that – and it hadn't been until recent years that the two sisters had even been in regular touch.

In a way, their mother's failing health had brought them together, but there was a strain between them – a sense of awkwardness that comes from unfamiliarity. The two women hardly knew each other.

Connie sat in the silence while Jean turned her attention back to making coffee. There was the harsh clatter of a spoon, the hiss of the boiling water, and then just the distant monotonous ticking of a clock... sounding like the prelude to something explosive.

Jean brought the cups to the table and slumped down in a chair with a sigh. She closed her eyes as if drawing on some inner reserve of strength. There was a loosening of her body, a relief. When she opened her eyes again she looked impossibly tired.

"How is work going?" Connie asked.

Jean's look said it all. She scraped her fingers through her hair. Her face seemed to collapse, becoming haggard. "The days are getting longer, the nights of rest shorter, and the money is stretching less than ever before," Jean admitted. She was an accountant, employed by a local firm.

Connie nodded, unwilling to continue with a conversation that would highlight her sister's frustration. The two women sat in stilted silence.

"You?"

Connie shrugged, said nothing. She was beginning to regret visiting. The bitterness and sadness of her sister's life seemed to drape itself around her shoulders like a cloak. She was a sad, lonely woman in a sad home. Connie felt sorry for her... until she realized that Jean's fortunes were little different from her own. That realization made her shake off her melancholy and force a smile onto her face and hope into her voice.

She reached for the briefcase. It was old, battered around the edges like a tradesman's well-worn tool. The black leather had been stripped off the handle. Connie squeezed the latches and the sound of the brass tabs snapping open on their springs was as loud as twin gunshots in the fragile silence. Jean flinched.

Connie reached her hand inside for the first painting, and then paused. She flicked a glance across the table to Jean and then took a deep breath.

"I withdrew two thousand dollars from the nursing home joint account when I was in Maine," she said. "I used the money to buy something."

For a long moment Jean sat perfectly still, and then a look of appalling horror came over her face. She began to shake her head in slow, numbed disbelief.

"Connie... that money..." the words faltered.

Connie nodded. "I know," she said. "It was the money for the next payment at the nursing home. But I bought something, Jean – something that will mean you will never have to worry about money for mom's care ever again."

She laid the first little painting out on the table, turned it around so Jean could see the beautiful colors, the exquisite craftsmanship that had gone into rendering the delicate gem of art. Connie's eyes were alight and she waited to see the spark of understanding and joy come into her sister's gaze.

Jean lifted her head slowly. Her eyes were dead.

She looked at Connie aghast – as though she had just come to her having spent all of their money on something as fanciful as a handful of magic beans.

"You..." Jean's voice faltered, wavered and then came back, "You paid two thousand dollars for... for this?"

Connie shook her head. Jean was staring at her white-faced. "No. I paid three thousand dollars for two paintings. I have one more here in the briefcase. I used the last thousand dollars I had, and the money from the account."

Connie laid the second, larger painting on the table. "They're Blake McGrath originals!"

Jean sat back slowly in her chair and tears of despair ran down her cheeks. Her face seemed to crumple, her shoulders sagged as though her tenuous grip on life had at last slipped and the misery that was her desperate existence suddenly overwhelmed her.

"Can you get your money back?" she sobbed. "Connie? Will the person give us our money back?"

Connie shook her head, saw the tortured pain in her elder sister's eyes. She reached across the old table and clasped at Jean's hands. "These are original Blake McGrath's," Connie said again with more emphasis. "Together, they're worth close to half a million dollars, Jean!"

Her sister looked blank and disbelieving at her through the smudge of her tears and there was nothing Connie could do to console her or convince her. She got up from the table, looked down at the forlorn figure of Jean one last time, and then made listless excuses to be away from her. "I'm tired from the driving. I think I'll go to bed."

As she lay in bed that night, Connie could hear her sister weeping softly through the thin walls.

In the morning, Jean moved listless as a ghost as Connie went out through the front door and set the suitcase and the briefcase in the trunk of her car. She came back to Jean then.

"I know you think I'm a fool," Connie said, "And I know you don't approve of the way I have lived my life – the choices I have made or the decisions I have made. But I am right about the paintings, Jean. And if all goes as planned, by this time tomorrow, you will never need to worry about the cost of mom's care ever again." She gazed into Jean's eyes, hoping she could reach her with the force of her voice and the earnestness in her eyes. "Just trust me. Just this once, trust me to know what I am doing."

Jean said nothing.

19.

Connie rode the elevator up to the offices above the art gallery with the briefcase held across her hips, both hands clutching tightly to the worn handle. She was shaking – literally trembling in her shoes. She was tired and grimy from the long drive back to New York that had taken most of the day, but now that fatigue and exhaustion had suddenly been shed by her fear of confrontation – for she knew too well what a cunning and malicious man Duncan Cartwright was.

She stepped off the elevator into a small plush carpeted lobby. The doors to Duncan's office were closed, but the door across from it – the one that opened into the boardroom – was ajar. She could hear the murmur of voices from within. Connie took a deep breath, raised her fist to knock... and then impulsively pushed the door wide open instead and went striding into the room, her shoulders back and jaw set with grim resolve.

Seated at the head of the boardroom table was Duncan, reclined and elegantly relaxed in a big leather chair, while across from him two older men stood respectfully facing him. One of the men was heavy in the shoulders, his suit polished shiny at the elbows, his tie awry around his neck. He was very old, Connie realized. He had spectacles perched on the end of his nose, his complexion florid with anxiety.

Beside him was another elderly man, overweight in an ill-fitting suit that seemed too small for him. The man was in mid-sentence, his rusty voice rising in some querulous protest. The words died on the man's slack lips as Connie strode wordlessly past them.

Duncan turned in his chair, smooth as a leopard that had spotted prey and did not wish to startle it. His eyes glittered with sly amusement, and something darker and malevolent that made Connie shudder. He flicked his gaze to the two elderly men and dismissed them with a scowl. They fled from the room and Duncan waited, the unruffled smile on his face frozen, until he heard the click of the door latch and knew for certain they were alone and would not be interrupted.

"Darling, you got my emails."

Connie nodded. "I got them," she said, "But I didn't open them."

Duncan arched his eyebrow in a parody of surprise. "Really?" he said. "Then why are you here? Why aren't you still traipsing up and down the coast of Maine, enjoying your vacation?"

"I came back early," Connie's mouth pinched. "I have something to show you." Without another word she set the briefcase down on the gleaming boardroom table and left it there as a taunt.

Slowly, Duncan rose to his feet and stepped away from the chair. There was an antique counter against a wall with bottles of alcohol and tumblers on a silver tray. He poured himself a drink and then offered a glass to Connie in a silent gesture. She gave a curt shake of her head.

Duncan splashed cubes of ice into the glass, swirled the contents, and then sipped thoughtfully. He glanced at Connie over his shoulder. "Do you mind if I smoke?" he asked with feigned courtesy.

She shrugged her shoulders. Duncan lit a cigar and puffed contentedly for several seconds until the tip glowed. At last, he turned around to Connie, and they faced each other across the small space that separated them.

For the first time in many months Connie stepped outside of herself and viewed Duncan with eyes that were dispassionate – unaffected. He had become gaunt, she saw. His eyes were sunken, and below them there were smudges of some ordeal, like swollen bruises. His fingers were never still, and there were new creases chiseled around his mouth that had been unseen until now.

"The photos of the painting you emailed me – it is a genuine McGrath," Duncan said, and his smile became oily. "But you knew that, didn't you?"

Connie nodded. Her lips were pressed thin and pale together so the words were little more than a whisper. "I told you. You didn't believe me."

Duncan nodded and held his arms out wide in a disarming gesture of surrender. "And you were right," he admitted ruefully. "So where is the painting... or is that what you have hidden in your briefcase?" His eyes flicked back to the table.

"That painting isn't for sale," Connie said. "I told you that too."

Duncan threw back his head and laughed, and the sound of his voice had a slightly jagged edge to it. "Well, maybe you're not quite persuasive enough," he said, his eyes glittering. "Money talks, darling, and I happen to have enough of it to make a very loud noise indeed." He paused then, gnawed on his lip and watched her over the rim of the glass. "Where is it?" he asked again.

"I'm not telling you," Connie's voice cracked, but she held his gaze with defiance.

Duncan shook his head and made a disappointed face. "You will," he said with an edge of menace, then grinned. It twisted his mouth. "Because if you don't, I will phone the bank and cut off your mother's nursing home money. Then I will have you thrown out of the apartment I am paying for, then I will –"

Connie wheeled on him, her face suddenly a snarl. She thrust out a finger of accusation at him and Duncan flinched. He had seen her eyes and been shocked at what they had revealed. There had been a blaze of pure hatred unveiled – an inscrutable and merciless glare that he had not expected. It was gone in an instant, hidden so swiftly that it might have been an illusion.

"No!" Connie hissed. "No more threats, Duncan. No more, not ever again. Tonight it is my turn to threaten you," she bristled.

Duncan set down the glass, all pretense of urbane charm burned away. He stood, mocking and belligerent, swaying on the balls of his feet. "Give it your best shot," he said.

Connie went to the table and opened the briefcase. She laid down the first, smallest painting, and pushed it towards him so that it glided across the smooth surface. Duncan glanced at it – and froze.

He shot a glare at Connie. "You found others?"

Connie nodded carefully. "I bought the last two seascapes available," she said. "This one I am giving to you, Duncan... in exchange for a waiver of all debts between us, all responsibilities, all sense of obligation. You get the painting, and I get to walk away from you and my guilt. No more will I have to cringe under your touch or feel revolted when you are too close to me. You take this painting and everything personal that existed between us is dissolved."

Duncan narrowed his eyes. He picked up the painting carefully and saw the signature, then turned it over and read the handwritten message that had been penciled on the back of the canvas. He turned to Connie and his eyes were monstrous.

"You found him!"

Connie said nothing. Duncan spun on his heel and went pacing across the boardroom, prowling like a lion. His jaws were chewing thoughtfully and there was a fine sheen of sweat across his forehead. He came back to Connie at last, and gripped at her hands.

"Work with me!" he said, gazing into her eyes, suddenly brimming with enthusiasm and charm. His voice was filled with an effusive passion that seemed to light the dark corners of the room. "Think of it, Connie!" he exclaimed. "It would be the exhibition to end all exhibitions. Imagine the publicity. A new Blake McGrath show. Together – you and me – we could make it happen."

Connie's face filled with loathing. "Go to hell," she hissed through clenched teeth. "And for the record, Duncan, that dedication is dated five years ago. That's no proof Blake McGrath is still alive, or that I found him."

"Liar!" Duncan roared. He lashed out and slapped Connie across her face with his open hand.

"I don't need proof," he roared maliciously. "It's in your eyes!"

Connie's head snapped to the side and a livid red mark burned on her cheek. She was pale with shock. She felt the sting of tears prickle in her eyes. Duncan stood over her, breathing hard, his rage seething. He clenched his hands, and then hammered his fists on the desk.

Slowly, carefully measuring each step, Connie went silently back to the brief case. "Do we have a deal for the painting?" she asked. Her voice had turned to ice.

Duncan threw his head back. She could see the veins in his neck standing thick as corded rope and his skin seemed to burn until it was red and swollen. "Yes," he snapped.

Connie nodded. She wanted to press her hand to her cheek, to salve the sting with the cool of her palm, but instead she reached into the briefcase again, and Duncan's eyes suddenly slammed back into focus.

"There is another painting," Connie said simply. "I am offering it to you for purchase." She set the second painting down on the table and closed the lid of the briefcase. "If you do not agree to my terms immediately, I will not hesitate to take it to another gallery in the morning."

There were little bubbles of spittle at the corner of Duncan's lips. He wiped his mouth on the back of his hand, and took a long deep breath to compose himself. He reached for the canvas, and his eyes became as sensual as a lover's caress. The painting was breathtaking. Duncan felt a fierce bewitched rise of passion and knew that he must own it – at any price.

"What do you want?" he growled.

"I want the sum of two hundred and ninety thousand dollars transferred into the account for my mother's ongoing care, and I want a further five thousand, five hundred dollars in cash. Right now."

Duncan's face registered his disbelief. "Are you serious?"

"Deadly serious," Connie said. "It's a fair price. The painting is signed, and it's the first new original work by the artist to come onto the market in a year." To demonstrate her resolve, she reached for the painting to take it away from him, but Duncan could not bear to be parted from it. He slammed his hand down impulsively. "Alright!" he spat.

Connie stood quite still. For several seconds she did not move and there was just the sound of Duncan's hoarse rasping breath. "I said now," Connie prodded him like antagonizing a dangerous wounded animal.

Duncan flinched. Cold hateful retribution blazed in his eyes, but he stalked to a phone and stabbed at the numbers. He gave instructions to his secretary to issue the payment to the nursing home account, and then flung open a drawer of the liquor cabinet so violently that the bottles clinked and teetered. He threw three bundles of cash carelessly across the big table. "There's six thousand," he said and his eyes lit with cruelty. "Not a lot of cash for a whore."

Connie put the money in the briefcase. Her hands were shaking, and a rise of nausea and relief washed over her like the burn of a fever. She felt herself sway with vertigo.

Duncan was watching her carefully. "Tell me," he taunted in a wheedling voice. "Now that we've completed our transaction... how did you get the paintings?"

Connie shook her head, and her dark hair swished across her shoulders. "We haven't completed our transaction until I confirm the money is in the nursing home account. That's when you will get the second painting."

Duncan stood back, gestured at the phone. He had composed himself now. His voice was deceptively calm, but Connie had lived through so many of his temper-driven storms she knew the respite would be brief. "Call," he invited.

Connie went warily to the phone and dialed her sister's number. She waited, grim-faced, until she heard Jean's voice.

"Jean. It's Connie. I need you to check the account balance for the nursing home," she said. There was a brief pause, and then Connie's voice became insistent. "Just do it – please."

Connie stared at Duncan, watching the man as he pored over the painting, his face a mask of rapture. After another long moment she nodded her head and hung up, Jean's joyous voice of incredulous amazement ringing like an echo in her ears.

"Satisfied?" Duncan looked up at her and asked. "Now, tell me where you got the paintings."

"I bought them."

He laughed cruelly. "I bet you did," he drew his eyes cynically down her body and the wrench of his lips became lazy disdain. "What did you use to pay for them? You don't have any money. Did you whore yourself out – spread your legs and close your eyes while he grunted on top of you?" He looked at her with contempt, like she was cast-off and somehow sullied. "Did you show him some of the tricks I taught you – thrill him with that talented mouth and body?"

Connie felt the scald of her revulsion burn the back of her throat. "Not every man has the same low gutter morals that you do, Duncan. Some men with honor still exist."

She spun on her heel, desperate for the door, and snatched up the briefcase. Duncan's voice called after her, rising strident with his fury. "You're finished in New York!" he screamed. "Finished! You'll never work in this town again."

Connie stopped in the doorway, turned back and forced an enigmatic smile to her lips that she knew would infuriate the man more than anything. "That's fine," she said. "I don't plan on being in New York for more than another day anyhow."

Connie pulled the boardroom door quietly closed behind her and strode to the elevator. The steel doors whispered shut, and as they did, she slumped down to the cold floor, weak, exhausted, and vulnerable. She was trembling with relief. Her shoulders began to shake uncontrollably, and at last the tears she had fought so hard to hold back came spilling down her cheeks, scalding her eyes.

20.

Connie woke the next morning in her tiny apartment and realized instinctively that she no longer belonged there. The noise of the city outside her window was like a nagging headache – a sound she had become so accustomed to now grated – and the need to be away from New York was like an itch that irritated beneath her skin.

She spent time on the phone, listened to her sister sob more happy joyful tears, and then asked Jean to transfer forty thousand dollars of the money Duncan had paid into her own account. That would leave a quarter of a million to cover the ongoing costs of their mother's nursing home care. The burden of responsibility that had buried Jean's life in a misery of work and worry had been forever lifted.

Then Connie called the movers, arranged to have the few bulky items she owned put into storage, and began to pack what she could carry downstairs to the trunk of her car.

The apartment was leased in Duncan's name and Connie had no doubt that he had already taken vindictive steps to have her removed. She wanted to be gone, away from him and the cloying odors of smog and fumes – away from the destructive memories of her life with him.

Her heart was calling her.

Connie had never considered herself a lover of the ocean. She had spent her childhood in the Midwest. Vacations to the coast had been infrequent, and never special. But now the salty air, the cleansing breeze, and the unbridled majesty of the waves was like a haunting siren of the sea, beckoning her with a sound that seemed to touch at her very soul.

She had driven more miles in the last few days than she could ever recall. She climbed behind the wheel one last time – and that knowledge was enough to compel her.

One last time.

She was heading north, back to Maine, not merely to start her life over again...

She was starting anew.

21.

By the time Connie crossed the bridge back into Hoyt Harbor, night had fallen, and the waterfront promenade was lit with a string of gaily-colored lights. There were crowds of vacationers on the foreshore gathered beneath a sky filled with stars, enjoying the balmy breeze that whispered across the rippling velvet of the harbor. Connie drove slowly past and found herself smiling, as though the vibrations of the night were somehow infectious.

She was paid up for another week at the vacation house she had rented, so she pulled wearily into the driveway. The car seemed to give a groan of relief, and Connie climbed from behind the wheel, stiff as an old woman. Her eyes were blurred, her mind numbed by the endless hours, and yet she couldn't help but feel her spirits lift. She stood for a moment, and just let herself be carried by the sense of elation that washed over her. But there was also a trace of fear, like menacing rocks that lurked beneath calm water. This was a new life, and it came with no promises, no guarantees. All she had to carry her along was her dream of her own little gallery.

"Uncertainty is just another word for adventure," she told herself bravely.

She had an unbidden image then – a vision of Blake McGrath that seemed to swirl in the fog of her weary imagination. And like tendrils of mist, he was impossible to hold; an enigmatic mystery that eddied in her mind, never quite leaving, but never entirely filling out, becoming vivid. All she could remember clearly was the man's smile.

She was still thinking about him when she curled up in bed and fell into the black death-like sleep of exhaustion.

22.

When the doors to the grocery store opened at 9am the following morning, Connie was waiting on the steps amidst a small group of tourists who had gathered in need of milk and bread or newspapers. She went straight to a pretty young girl behind one of the cash registers and asked to speak to Warren Ryan.

He came to the front of the store after just a few minutes, already looking harried. When he saw Connie there was a spark of instant recognition, followed by a flicker of trepidation in his eyes. His steps faltered, and then he came on with something like grim concern.

"Hello," he said. "Nice to see you again. Is everything all right?" He had already spent the money Connie had paid for the paintings, clearing up pressing debts with suppliers and placating the banks. Now his features were pale with dread.

"No," Connie said. She looked up into the man's face. "I need to speak with you in private. It's about those paintings."

Ryan's shoulders slumped. "Miss, I'm sorry, but we had an –"

Connie cut him off. "Please," she insisted. "I assure you, what I have to say will only take a minute."

Ryan trudged down the long aisles like a man on his way to the gallows, and went heavily up the steps to his office with Connie close behind him. She sat across from his desk, and Ryan dropped into his chair. He flicked on the desk lamp and then his eyes seemed to furtively search the room as though looking for a concealed escape.

"When I paid you three thousand dollars for the two paintings I purchased, I did so based on my impressions of their value," Connie began politely. She was enjoying herself. Behind her reserved demeanor and calm tone was a gleeful delight that she worked hard to suppress. "Well, it turns out that wasn't the case..."

Ryan bounced up from his chair as though he had been waiting for this moment to launch into his defense. He shook his head, hitched up his sagging trousers, and propped his hands on his hips. "We arrived at a fair price," the man's voice rose an octave and became insistent. "You saw the paintings – you... you even made a phone call. I was happy with the agreement and, let me say, you were happy with the agreement also."

Connie nodded. "But that was before I had an understanding of their fair value," she smiled sweetly and at last she let the twinkle of pleasure reach her eyes. "That's why I want to write you a check, Mr. Ryan. For an additional forty thousand dollars."

Warren Ryan's mouth fell open in disbelief. Dazedly he dropped down into his chair, and cuffed away tears that misted in his eyes.

23.

The road south along the coast looked very different to Connie as she put the car through a series of bends and sweeping curves. It was midday and the sun flickered through the tops of the pines and dappled the blacktop in shade and light.

She recalled the night of the storm, and passed fallen trees that had been dragged to the gravel shoulder. The memory of that night made her irrationally wary, and despite the perfect weather and the dry road, it was well over an hour of cautious driving before she finally saw the sign-posted turn off to Jellicat Road. Then, quite suddenly, a wave of fear and panic overwhelmed her.

She pulled off the road at the green mailbox and the car jounced along the dirt trail. Connie went only a hundred yards and then had to stop.

Her palms were sweating, and she was shaking like a leaf. She could feel every breath jag anxiously in her throat, and the beat of her heart was an erratic pounding. She got out of the car, surrounded by the dense press of woods, and stood in the still air, forcing herself to breathe, willing her body to relax. Through the long miles and longer days since they had first met, Connie had played out this moment in her imagination time and time again, until it had become so unaccountably significant that it had taken on the weight of a life-changing moment. She shook her head, annoyed.

Blake McGrath was just a man, she told herself.

As a distraction, she opened the trunk and drew the briefcase towards her. Slowly, she counted out five hundred dollars, and tucked the roll of bills into her pocket. She concealed the briefcase under a bundle of blankets she had brought from her apartment, and then closed the trunk.

Connie wandered a short way along the trail, hearing the distant percussive rumble of surf along the beach and the songful call of birds high up in the branches. There was a muddy puddle ahead of her and she stepped towards it. The water had shrunken under the baking heat of the sun so she could see a surround of dark wet dirt like an ebbing tide. She peered into the few inches of shallow water, made blue by the reflected sky. For a moment, all she could see were brown lumps of gravel, and then, quite miraculously, she was able to conjure up the image of Blake. He was smiling at her, his mouth in a quirky teasing grin and the corners of his eyes crinkling with pleasure. It was so clear, so vivid in every detail that she blinked, and took a step back. After a moment she peered into the puddle once more and tried to project Duncan's face, yet when she did, the surface of the puddle seemed rippled so that the pieces of her memory could never quite come together.

Connie got back behind the steering wheel and stared at her own face in the rearview mirror. She could see the nervousness in her reflection, and the smudges of fatigue that hung like soft shadows below her eyes. She practiced her smile, then tried to compose her features into an expression of cool and calm. She dabbed the tip of a finger at her lipstick, and abruptly decided the coral color was too much – too overt. She wiped her lips clean of paint and sighed a regret that she had chosen to wear a shirt and jeans instead of the pretty yellow dress left behind at the rental house. Finally in frustration, she slumped back in the seat, dark and brooding with confusion and turmoil.

"I should go back to Hoyt Harbor," she pouted her lips, and then just as quickly dismissed the idea. She had come this far, and there was a reason. For despite the clothes, the makeup and anything else she did, what could not be concealed was the transparent sparkle of eagerness in her eyes.

She simply *had* to see him again.

24.

Blake heard the crunch of tires on gravel and looked up with a puzzled frown from underneath the open hood of the old truck. His hands were black with grease. He plucked a dirty rag from his back pocket and wiped at them. The car pulled up just a few yards away and Connie stepped out into the bright sunshine.

His pleasure to see her again was transparent, and his smile a handsome welcome for her. Connie was suddenly very glad she had come. Blake straightened and drew the back of his hand across his forehead. He was sweating under the warm sun. The front of his shirt clung wet to the contours of his chest and Connie saw his chin was blued with a day's growth of stubble. She hooded her eyes and had a tantalizing image of him leaning close to kiss her, and then fantasized how his whiskers would feel bristling and electric against her cheek. She caught her breath.

"What a waste," she said.

Blake furrowed his brow.

"It's a beautiful day and you're working on a truck," she said around a warm smile. "Your hands were made for painting, and a day like this was made for swimming."

Blake nodded. "Well the truck won't fix itself," he said laconically. "And I don't paint any more. I don't go in the water, either."

Connie looked stunned, not understanding. "You live on a beautiful beach, and you don't go in the water?"

"That's right," Blake said with an edge of dry finality. He turned towards the house then and got to the porch steps before he glanced over his shoulder, back to where Connie was standing. "Come on," he said. "I need to wash my hands, and I don't think you drove all this way to talk about the beach. I feel like I'm going to need to be sitting down before I hear the rest of what you have to say." He smiled widely then, and the pleasure in his face smoothed away the edge to his words so that Connie was helpless to do anything other than to smile impishly back.

Connie came into the living room, her eyes adjusting to the shaded gloom while Blake went to the sink and scrubbed his hands. Ned was asleep on his bed. Connie crouched down and scratched the big dog behind his ear. Ned's eyes opened and the Great Dane yawned. He thumped his tail against the mattress and then rolled over. Connie scratched under the dog's chin and his huge brown eyes rolled back with pleasure.

When Blake returned to the living room he had cold drinks in either hand. He offered a glass to Connie and gestured for her to sit. She propped herself on the edge of the sofa like she was poised to take flight. Her eyes were bright and glittering.

"So..." Blake said. "I never thought I was going to see you again."

Connie smiled. She reached into her pocket and produced the roll of bank notes. She handed them across to Blake. "It's the five hundred dollars you loaned me," she explained. "I came to pay you back."

Blake nodded. He set the money aside and watched Connie as he sipped at his drink. She was beautiful in a way he couldn't describe. It was something intangible that transcended the physical appeal of her, he realized. It was something more — a special quality about her that seemed to make her body hum with a vitality and energy he found infectious. He lowered himself into the chair across from the sofa and spent a moment just admiring her, remembering every feature that he had burned into his memory. Artists, by training, have a keen eye for detail, and Blake compared his recollections of this young woman against the reality now that she was here again. Her nose was slim, and there was a sensuality about her mouth and chin that seemed to radiate inner strength and yet soft femininity. Her eyes were alive and bewitching, and her hair that hung down over her shoulders seemed to shimmer as she turned her head. She was very beautiful, but also very appealing, he decided. There was substance behind the stunning façade of face and figure.

"What are you thinking?" Connie asked at last, and Blake's thoughts came bubbling back to the surface like a drowning man reluctant to be saved.

"I was just thinking about your car," he concealed the truth. "Did you get it repaired?"

Connie nodded. "I took it to the mechanic at Hoyt Harbor," she said.

"And you sold both of the paintings, I assume?"

"Yes."

He lapsed back into reflective silence and Connie felt compelled to say something — to fill the contemplative void. "I also left New York," she blurted.

He arched his eyebrows in genuine surprise. "What about your job at the art gallery?"

"I kind of got fired," she confessed.

"Kind of?" Blake became bemused. "Why?"

Connie gestured with her hands. "It's a long story, but it basically boiled down to the fact that the gallery director wanted to know where you were living and how I came across the paintings. When I refused to tell him..."

"He fired you?"

She nodded.

"But you sold the paintings?"

"Yes."

"So you're right for money for many years to come, no doubt."

Connie shook her head. "No," she said. "I have five thousand dollars. The rest of the money from the sale went towards taking care of my mother, and I also gave Mr. Ryan at the grocery store more money for the paintings."

Blake sat back in the chair, taking everything in. He narrowed his eyes with curiosity. "So where are you living?"

Connie gave a bitter laugh of wry self-depreciation. "I have another week left in my vacation rental at Hoyt Harbor. After that," she shrugged. "I'll probably be sleeping in my car."

She paused and wondered if she had been too dramatic. She saw Blake's eyes become darker and there was a deepening scowl on his face.

She laughed the moment off lightly. "I'm sure I'll find somewhere to live," she said quickly. "It's the price I am willing to pay."

"Pay? For what?"

"For following my dream," Connie's voice became soft as a shy whisper. "My dream of owning a little art gallery somewhere here in Maine."

They stared at each other in the pointed silence. Connie's words hung in the air between them like an omen to the next stage of the conversation. Blake said nothing for a long time and then sat forward in the chair.

"There are two things that define a person," he said levelly. "Your patience when you have nothing, and your attitude when you have everything."

Connie watched Blake's mouth, listened to the deep rumble of his voice. She felt delicious little shivers dance up her spine. She understood the importance of what he was saying, but she wanted desperately to keep the atmosphere between them happy. She grinned. "Well I have nothing," she said, "And I'll try to be patient. Hopefully one day, I'll have everything and a good attitude to go with it."

Blake smiled despite himself, a wry curl of his lips. "Everything isn't necessarily measured in terms of money," he cautioned. "For some people, their everything is family and loved ones."

Connie nodded and glanced away. She had been shocked at how pleased she was to see him again, and how intensely she had missed being near this man. Her pulse was thumping like a drum in her ears. She plucked at the leg of her jeans and licked her lips, as though to bolster her reserves of determination.

When Connie glanced back, she saw that Blake was studying her with an intriguing look in his eyes that might have been amusement, or perhaps wariness.

Or maybe something else entirely.

The smile faltered on Connie's face, and she felt a hot flush of blood burn on her cheeks.

"Blake, I want to do an exhibition of your old paintings," she blurted before her resolve deserted her entirely. Her throat felt suddenly swollen, and the words came out in a choke. "I want to be your agent."

For a long tense moment Blake said nothing. His features seemed carved in stone. "I don't need an agent."

She nodded, took a deep breath. "But I need a client," she said at last. "And you told me to follow my dream and not let anyone stop me. So please," her face became pleading, "Give me this chance to turn my dream into reality."

Blake rose stony faced from the chair and walked wordlessly into the kitchen. Connie followed him with her eyes, her heart full of dread.

"Do you despise me?" she called to him softly. Her expression was stricken.

Blake turned back to her, left her question unanswered.

"What exactly did you have in mind?" he asked. His voice was flat.

"I would like to show your paintings – not sell them, nor profit from them. Just exhibit them, so that they can be seen."

"I wondered why you came back," he admitted, and then cut his words off, as though what he said

145

next was important and needed to be measured. "I had hoped it... it was for personal reasons."

Connie leaped up from her chair. There was too much space between them and she went to him, unsure of how he would react. She stood in the kitchen and her eyes became huge and somber.

"It was," she admitted. Her legs were trembling and she felt herself teeter. She clutched at the doorframe to hold herself upright. "I wanted to come back to see you."

He looked unconvinced. There was a cynical arch to his eyebrow. "And you wanted to get my permission to show the paintings."

Connie lowered her head and stared down at the floor. Her hair hung down over her face like a veil. She took a deep shuddering breath and felt as though she was on the edge of an abyss with the ground beneath her quickly crumbling away. She lifted her face at last and wrung her hands.

"I wanted to be near you," she said in a whisper. "Yes, I want to show your paintings – I won't deny that because the world deserves to enjoy them – *but coming back here and seeing you again was what mattered most.*" She stopped suddenly, worried that she had already said too much, but yearning to say more. So much more. She bit her lip as though to physically choke off the rush of impassioned words that leaped to her lips.

Connie saw some flicker of reaction behind Blake's eyes – a fissure in the stone of his expression.

"Blake...?"

Connie's words had seared like a white-hot brand across his mind. He felt a lightheaded lift that gripped at his heart and squeezed tight as a fist, and he wondered suddenly if his emotions were transparent – if she could see the feelings she stirred within him every time he looked at her.

He glanced away lest she saw that thing in his gaze which would leave him so vulnerable. "Let me think," he said gruffly.

He went out through the door without another word and Ned rose instinctively from his bed and trailed him down the porch steps. Blake walked stiffly down to the sand, stood for a long moment as the surf lapped around his feet, and then began to pace with his head bowed in thought towards the northern end of the beach.

He was in conflicted turmoil – unable to turn away from the realization that he had missed Connie, and that he had longed for her to return.

But he wondered, after all he had endured, whether his grief had left him susceptible, or if the loneliness of his existence had left his heart so dry and exposed that his tumbling emotions were merely an illusion of his solitude.

And with this woman, he knew, came guilt. He had encouraged her to pursue her dreams, and he felt some of the burden of her dilemma – the loss of her job for keeping the vow of secrecy he had sworn her to.

He stopped pacing suddenly, looked up and was startled to realize the trail of his footprints stretched the length of the beach and back again. Ned was splashing in the edge of the surf. The big dog came to him shaking water from his shoulders, his tongue hanging pink from his mouth.

After an hour he came back in through the doorway kicking sand from his feet with Ned like a shadow at his side. His face was creased and had been colored by the sun.

Connie was sitting pensively on the sofa, her hands clasped in her lap, her expression wracked with the appalling tension of a patient waiting in dread for a doctor's results. She looked up into his face as he stood there, a broad shouldered silhouette against the glare through the door.

"I will let you do an exhibition of my old paintings when you establish your gallery." He thrust a warning finger in the air and scowled, "But there is a condition."

Connie leaped from her chair, went to throw her arms impulsively around his neck and cover him with the bubbling joy of her kisses – but she stopped herself with a great effort, so that instead her move towards him was curtailed to an awkward wave of her arms and demure restraint. "Thank you," she gushed, certain that all she was feeling shone transparent. "I cannot tell you how grateful I am." Her face was lifted up to his and her lips were glossy and soft, her eyes flooded. Blake wanted to kiss those lips, to taste the sweetness of her. He drew a breath.

"There is a condition," he reminded her. She had come towards him and he had raised his arms to wrap them around her, his heart squeezed, wishing it to be so. But she had stopped, and the small space between them felt like a desolate ache.

"Condition?" Connie's cheeks were bright and behind the long dark lashes her eyes glittered like precious gems. "What condition?"

Blake made his face stern. "I want to paint you – I want to paint your portrait."

Connie went quite still, like some timid animal on the edge of a forest. She searched Blake's eyes in confusion.

"You want to paint me? But you don't paint... and you don't paint portraits."

"I want to try."

"How long would it take?"

Blake shrugged. In truth he didn't know. "Maybe two weeks," he considered. "Perhaps three. It's been a long time since I sat at an easel. I don't know how difficult it will be to get my technique back."

Connie was bewildered by the request, but secretly also elated by the idea. The chance to spend so much time with Blake was like a tantalizing promise.

"When would you want to make this painting?"

"As soon as possible," he said without hesitating. "But I would need to clean out the studio first. Maybe the day after tomorrow..."

"So soon?"

"Yes."

Connie nodded slowly, her mind trying to deal with the daunting logistics of driving from Hoyt Harbor each day, and the looming dilemma of housing. But she shrugged those issues aside and nodded her head. "Fine," she said.

He was pleased. She saw it on his face. "They will be long days," he felt compelled to caution her. "Have you ever sat for a portrait before?"

Connie giggled. "Of course not."

"Well we will be starting early and finishing late – I like to paint well into the night..." he stopped himself then, realized the sacrifice he was asking of her and tilted his head quizzically as a fresh, intriguing thought struck him. "Would you like to stay here – until the painting is finished, I mean? I have a spare room with an empty bed. You're welcome to it, and it would save you a lot of driving – a lot of time on the road..."

Connie didn't flinch. For just an instant she considered the offer and saw laid out before her a solution to everything her heart yearned for.

"Yes," she said solemnly and nodded her head. "If you just tell me why. Why you want to paint again after all this time, and why, of all people, you want to paint me."

Blake stood unmoving, a man whose grip on his private pain was slowly unraveling, and at last he had no choice but to let go, to fall. He weighed all that must be risked from laying bare his soul. His grief and his secrets were all he had that mattered, and the idea of opening himself up in such an intimate way chilled his blood.

"Connie, I'm going blind," he said at last. "And painting you is my last chance for redemption."

25.

"Blind?" Connie repeated the word and the sound of it seemed to pierce her heart as a shocking pain. She fell like dead-weight back onto the sofa.

Blake nodded his head soberly. "Yes," he said.

"Are you sure?"

"Yes," Blake said. "It's a hereditary condition, and it's progressive. I've known about it for many years."

Connie shook her head in slow disbelieving denial, her eyes like deep wells of despair. "Can anything be done?"

"No. Nothing at all."

Connie lapsed into silence, her emotions swirling. She went very still for a long time, her gaze vacant. Then suddenly the sickening pain of it came to her again, and a deep raw ache left her eyes brimming with tears.

She got slowly back to her feet and reached for Blake's hand. She squeezed his fingers tight in a convulsing spasm like some injured little thing and then her hand went very soft and still. "How long have you got before..?"

Blake shrugged. "I honestly don't know," he admitted. "I first noticed my vision blurring several years ago, but I thought nothing of it. I was young – I thought I was ten feet tall and bulletproof. But lately, it has become progressively worse. I'm losing close up focus, although my long-range vision seems fine. It's like my eyes are dying from the inside out."

He needed space. Connie was too close to him, and he felt the claustrophobia of her; the way she was looking up into his eyes with a tragic kind of sympathy that made him feel vaguely resentful. He didn't want compassion – he wanted her to understand

He backed away, let her hand slide through his fingers and went to the bookcase. "That's why I'm reading so much," he admitted. "And that's why I want to paint you, Connie. It may be my last chance to make a painting. I know one day – sooner or later – I'm going to wake up blind."

She stood, desolate in the middle of the living room, fighting back the need to weep. She nodded her head, and then recalled how he had pressed his face close to the two canvases when he had signed them for her. She clenched her hands into tiny fists and felt a rash of cold clammy sweat break out across her body.

"I understand," she said.

"So you still want to sit for my painting?"

"Yes, of course."

Blake was relieved. He bowed his head and for many moments just peered down at the rug-covered floor. When he looked up again, his face had changed, becoming somehow vulnerable and wounded. His eyes had the empty hollow cast of dark despair, as though he had stepped into a deep shadow.

"Sometimes," he said softly, "I close my eyes and imagine what it will be like." There was a whisper of anguish woven between his words. "I try to walk through the house with my eyes closed, groping for the walls, stumbling over pieces of furniture..." he shook his head suddenly overcome by his embarrassment, and turned blinking to stare out of the window.

Connie felt the yearning need to go to him, but she sensed that was not what he wanted. She stood very still and stared his broad back, watched the rise and fall of his shoulders as he took deep breaths.

"I don't know what I'll do about Ned," Blake seemed to be speaking to the distant ocean. "I know it's going to happen – I know I'm going to be blind one day – but I just can't seem to come to terms with it, or prepare myself."

"It might not happen for many years," Connie offered in a consoling whisper.

Blake turned. "I wish you were right," he said and fought to keep self-pity from his tone. "But it's coming, Connie. I can sense it. One day in the near future, I'm going to find myself alone in a world of darkness that I can't ever truly be prepared for."

26.

Sunset came as a sudden surprise – they had talked through the afternoon, and it was only when Ned rose from his bed, stiff through his hind legs, that Blake seemed to recognize the painted riot of color that was spread across the setting sky. The big dog stood quietly waiting. Blake went through the kitchen and disappeared for a moment. When he returned he had a single red rose in his hand. He looked solemnly at Connie, torn for just an instant.

"We're going down to the beach," he said quietly. "We go there every day at this time. You're welcome to come along if you like. It's just a moment Ned and I share... but if you're going to be staying here," his voice trailed off to a toneless whisper, "you might as well know."

She followed them down to the beach, watching man and dog walk slowly across the sand and down to the water's edge, keeping her distance, leaving them to the intimate bond that seemed to drape around the two lonely figures like a cloak of grief.

It was cold. The breeze off the ocean was frigid, and the ocean without a blue sky above it had begun to turn slate grey as the waves rolled hissing and rumbling towards the beach. Connie wrapped her arms around herself and hugged her shoulders. The wind tugged at her hair and pulled errant tendrils from the bind of her ponytail.

She stood in silence and saw Blake lift his face to the tangerine clouds, stained by the bleeding color of the sun's last light. Then he lowered his head to the rose, kissed the crimson petals, and waded into the surf until the white water was dashing against his knees. He threw the rose beyond the breaking line of the first wave and then came back to the sand and stood sadly beside the big dog until the tide drew the rose away, into the ocean's icy embrace.

Blake stood stiffly, reached a hand down for the dog and patted the Great Dane's head. Ned barked once, then fell silent. The sounds of the ocean seemed to rise and then softly sigh.

It was almost dark when at last they turned away from the sea and came slowly back up the beach. Connie noticed Blake's eyes were red rimmed and swollen.

27.

"If there is a God, I believe he is a vengeful one," Blake said slowly. He was seated at the small kitchen table, with Connie sitting quietly across from him. Between them were the remains of cold meat slices that had been eaten in strained gloomy silence.

Connie looked up into Blake's face with an expression of surprise.

"What do you mean?"

Blake rose slowly from his chair, took the plates to the sink, then began pacing. He was frowning. Connie watched him as he took carefully measured steps like his feet were moving to the beat of some thumping sound echoing in his mind. The night suddenly became still, as if infused with an eerie heaviness, so that the only sound seemed to be the dull press of Blake's shoes on the old timber floorboards.

Connie followed him with her eyes, twisting in her chair as he prowled the living room floor. He reached out absently and ran his fingers across the spines of the paperback novels on a bookshelf and then stopped at last, somehow dark despite being lit by all the blazing lights throughout the house. He sighed, and Connie sensed that at last he was ready to talk. She leaned forward attentively with her elbows propped on her knees and her chin cupped between her hands. She sensed the need to stay silent – to listen without interruption lest he lapse into silence, and yet, despite herself, she wanted to spare him the pain of explanation.

"Blake," she said in a whisper, "It's okay. You don't have to tell me anything if you don't want to... if fact I think I already know what you have been trying to say."

Connie had always had an inkling of the dark tragedy that had changed his life, she realized – some preternatural sense, drawn from the paintings she had seen with the beautiful young woman, and his sudden decision to stop painting, to disappear from the world. She rose slowly, but kept her distance, not wanting to intrude, but needing to reach out to him with her understanding.

"Somewhere in your past, you lost the young woman you loved, and she was your muse. It's the reason you gave up painting, and it's the reason you go down to the beach each night," Connie's eyes became solemn and sad for him. Her face was very pale, her lips trembling. "She's the woman in the paintings I saw."

Blake looked haunted – a ghostly apparition that stood unmoving, with his features somehow blasted and eroded by the sudden heart wrenching pain that welled in his eyes. He stared at Connie, his gaze seeming to pass right through her, as though he was peering emptily at another time, another place.

"I have been given two gifts in my life," his voice was raw and rusty, somehow detached from the man himself. "Two great loves. The first was painting. The second was my daughter, Chloe, who died when she was just six years old."

Connie froze. An icy pall draped itself over her so that she could not breath, could only stare in horror.

"She drowned on that beach," Blake said, his voice beginning to break into soft chokes as he fought back the sting of burning tears. "She drowned five years ago." He moved away as though seeking darkness, his eyes suddenly haunted by the nightmares of his past. The timbre went from his voice until each word was flat and listless, devoid of color or emotion.

"When I was making my way through the art world – before I broke into the major galleries – I met a girl and we moved in together. We weren't in love, we were just comfortable with each other's company. Then, by happy accident, my daughter Chloe was born and my career began to take off. She was about to start school when I held my last exhibition in New York. We decided to move here. I wanted to be by the sea, I wanted to draw daily on the inspiration of the ocean for my next collection of paintings, so we came here to Maine, bought a dog, and I began painting for a show that would never happen..."

Blake moved like a shadowy specter, the light in the living room now directly over his head so that the strong broad of his brow turned his eyes into dark hollow sockets.

"One day I was working in the studio. Ned was still a pup, and he was curled up in a corner. The woman," he could not bring himself to mention her name, "was on the beach with Chloe, playing in the surf line. It was sunset..."

He couldn't go on. He just fell silent for long moments, the tragedy of that moment playing over and over in his mind like an unimaginable nightmare. He heard the screams, the cries of panic and horror and then saw himself again running blindly through the house, his face white with shock, stumbling down onto the darkening beach with Ned at his heels. He saw the woman, her head buried in her hands and then realized...

Blake had blundered into the surf, screaming for Chloe, thrashing amongst the waves sobbing with fear, crying out until his throat was hoarse, until his legs could hold him no more.

"It's why Ned and I go down to the beach at sunset and send a rose out into the sea," he said at last. "And it's why Ned goes every night to sit and wait on the empty beach until the sun comes up. He's waiting for Chloe."

Connie was crying, her face slick with heartbroken tears that fell like rain from her cheeks. She felt a choke of emotion in her throat so that every breath was a sobbing gasp. "The light house..." she said softly in understanding.

Blake nodded. "I leave the lights on, because I want Chloe to be able to find her way home, to find her way back to me," he said helplessly.

"But the woman in the paintings?"

"Chloe," Blake admitted. "I took five paintings and I added a beautiful raven-haired young woman to them. It was how I imagined her – how I pictured she might look if she had ever grown up. I sent the paintings out into the world in the hope that one day she might see them, see herself in one of my paintings and know that she was remembered... and loved..."

Connie felt broken – utterly destroyed. She could not stop the tears that burned in her eyes. Never had she imagined this man had held so much

159

sadness within him, coveting it and holding it so close to him that like a destructive fire, it had burned away his heart and soul. She took a tentative step towards him, but Blake seemed to flinch from her. She stopped, went quiet again, sniffing back more tears and aching just to take him in her arms so that he could weep without shame, without reserve. Her lips were apart, quivering with grief.

"I thought God was vengeful," Blake said. His shoulders were slumped now, his shape made gaunt and shrunken. He cuffed brusquely at tears that shone on his cheeks. "I thought I was being punished for not appreciating Chloe enough, not loving her enough, not being a good father. He took her from me because I was immersed in my art."

He heaved a deep shuddering breath that was the sound of impossible sorrow.

"After Chloe drowned, I could never paint the ocean again. The sea had given me a career, and then she had turned cruelly on me and taken the life of my daughter. So I gave up my art, and turned my back on the world. And now it seems that once again God has come seeking revenge. I have ignored my gift, and as punishment he is making me blind." Blake seemed to slump at the cruel irony of fate, and at last fell silent, spent and grieving, like the pain poured from his soul in an open wound that could never be healed.

Connie took another step closer, and this time he did not flinch, did not move away.

"You can still paint."

"For now."

"And you blame God?"

Blake fell silent again. He glanced at Connie, but couldn't hold her gaze. He fled to the window and stared for a long time out at the shadows of the dark night. He was shaking his head slowly.

"Maybe I didn't love Chloe enough," he said so softly, the words so tortured that Connie barely heard him. "Maybe I didn't appreciate her, or cherish her. Maybe I stopped deserving her... and so she was taken from me."

"Do you believe that?"

"I don't know," the words were wrung from him. "But if it was because I failed her, and if I'm going blind because I turned my back on my gift in the same way I didn't appreciate Chloe, then I need to find a way to square my soul, find some peace."

"The portrait?"

"My salvation," he said with the sudden conviction that could only come from desperate, despairing belief.

28.

Connie went down the porch steps and stood peering into the gloom of the night. The wind was gusting, shredding dark clouds across the moon so that the world seemed bathed in a soft glow without edges or definition.

She followed the path down to the beach and when she reached the sand she turned back suddenly and saw the bright lights ablaze in the house – a sad, sorrowful reminder of a little girl lost, disguised by the warm and welcoming glow of a beacon.

Her steps became heavy as she walked towards the lonely shape of the dog, sitting patiently above the high tide line. Ned was black as the night, seemingly carved from the same craggy dark rocks of the headland. He turned, saw Connie coming towards him and recognized her.

Connie dropped into the sand beside the dog and threw her arm up, around the Great Dane's shoulder.

They sat in companionable silence, the big dog gazing with sad eyes at the blackness of the ocean, and Connie watching the white phosphorous explosions of foam as the waves hissed and dashed upon the shore. She sighed, and scratched her fingers down Ned's back. He was like a shelter against the wind, an anchor to her worried thoughts that formed in her mind like waves but then burst apart before she could analyze or understand them.

"Ned, what am I going to do?" Connie spoke out loud, her words whipped away on the breeze. "Everything tells me I should go – that Blake's fallen too deep into his own despair for me to reach him... and yet... and yet I am hopelessly attracted to him."

She wrapped her fingers around a handful of sand and let it trickle from her grip as if poured through an hourglass. It was like life, she decided as she watched the tiny grains spill like flakes of gold. There was only a handful of time to live life, to savor its joys and disappointments, its agony and ecstasy. She thought about that time slipping her by, and then suddenly instead considered all the sand still in her hand – what remained in her grasp. It seemed to Connie to be the answer she was seeking.

She leaned against Ned, resting her head against his shoulder. She could hear the deep sonorous sound of his breathing, a steady rhythm like the ebb and hiss of the waves.

"I'll stay," she said.

She got to her feet slowly, scratched Ned behind his ears and stared one final time out at the empty black void of the ocean. Then she turned on her heel and walked back up the beach towards the house. There was still sand clinging between her fingers to remind her that time and hope were still in her hands.

29.

Blake was standing in the hallway entrance when Connie came through the screen door. He was bare-chested, wearing only denim jeans that were slung low at his hips. He had a towel in his hand, his dark hair curling and wet, and his chest tanned the color of old oak.

He draped the towel over his shoulder. "Did you find what you were looking for?"

Connie felt a flush of warmth across her cheeks and a prickling of the fine dark hairs at the nape of her neck. Her breath caught for an instant in the back of her throat. She wanted to stare, felt obliged to look away – and in the end did nothing except stammer in confusion.

"Pardon?"

"You said you were going to your car to find something when I went for a shower. I was just wondering if you found what you were looking for?" There was no taunt on Blake's face, no understanding of the effect he was having on her. Connie managed a rattled little smile

"Yes," she said quickly and found distraction by brushing the sand from her hands. "And then I went down to the beach."

Blake nodded, going back down the hall towards the bedroom and Connie let out the breath that had strangled in her throat. When he came back he had stretched on a t-shirt, and Connie's legs were no longer trembling.

"It's too late now for you to drive back to Hoyt Harbor," Blake offered. "I thought I might sleep on the sofa again. You're welcome to the bed."

Connie frowned. "I don't want to inconvenience you," she protested. "You said you had a spare bed?"

Blake nodded and his eyes flicked away, down the hallway in the direction of the studio. "It's in Chloe's room," he said and Connie was surprised that the words were not bruised by the lingering ache of his sadness. "I was going to clean the room out for you tomorrow, while I was organizing the studio."

Connie nodded, sensed another change in the man, like the first hint of the sun breaking through on an overcast day. There was warmth there now, still watery and weak, but better than the dark brooding clouds. She smiled. "I don't want to be any trouble," she said abstractly, but Blake seemed to understand.

"Chloe's things are all packed in boxes, the closet is empty. I just need to scrape away five years of dust," then his voice lowered and became filled with meaning. "You're no trouble. The room is yours for as long as you want it or need it."

Connie felt herself melt a little in the sudden warmth, and she thought desperately of a way to feed that flicker of life she saw glint faintly in his eyes. They talked about art, its rich history and the movements that had emerged through the twentieth century, until slowly the stiffness went from his voice as she coaxed him with a covert thrill as he began to warm and then relaxed.

"Can you tell me more about the portrait you're planning?" she asked.

Blake inclined his head. "I want to paint you in sunlight," he said, and Connie sensed that he was scrolling through images in his mind, visualizing then discarding again until an idea began to firm and he groped towards it. "Near the window sill," he said. "Some of the most beautiful paintings by the old masters were studies in light. I want to do the same thing – create a painting that pays tribute to the greats of the past, but in a way that makes the work timeless."

Connie smiled. "I saw a painting like that once," she said softly, not wanting to shatter the fragility of the mood, nor distract him from his vision. "It was in Amsterdam. It inspired my passion for art."

They went down the hallway and stood together in the studio, suddenly like renovators mapping out grand plans with animated waves of their arms as they shared ideas and thoughts.

"I'll move the easel," Blake said. "Maybe that bench as well," he added. His eyes were narrowed, scheming, understanding the intricacies of the process and seeing the room, not as it was, but how it must be. "And then I'll have you standing here," he gripped her lightly by the shoulders, moved her on shuffling feet like a mannequin until she was positioned at the window, leaning on the wooden sill and staring out into the blackness.

Connie glanced sideways at him. "Where will you paint me from?"

Blake took a couple of steps away from her, his eyes everywhere at once. "Here," he said decisively, and he scraped his heel across the old floorboards, making a faint mark through the film of grey dust. "The light will spill across your face and your arms and then filter across the far wall, fading gradually."

"Props?" Connie asked.

Blake blinked. He hadn't considered the possibility. He thought for a moment, and then shook his head. "No, it needs to be you – your face, your shoulders. Nothing else matters. Anything more and the painting will become confused.

"What should I wear? What about jewelry?"

"Do you have any?"

That made Connie arch her eyebrows in uncertainty. She had a jewelry box. It was buried under blankets and clothes in the trunk of the car, but nothing expensive, nothing exquisite enough for a painting. She shook her head slowly. "No," she said at last. "Nothing that would be worth painting."

Blake nodded. It wasn't important. The more he played the vision in his mind, the more he understood the need for simplicity. "I'll need to paint your bare shoulders," he said and drew a line across his own chest, level with his armpits, using the flat edge of his hand.

"You want me topless?" Connie's voice was a panicked squeak.

"No," Blake reassured her. "But maybe in a bra, with the straps off your shoulders. Would you be comfortable with that?"

Connie's eyes became glazed for a moment of modesty, and then she gave a little shrug of her shoulders. "Yes."

Blake grabbed at the easel, set it on the mark he had scraped across the floor, and then went striding purposefully across to the rack where the rows of canvases were stored. He ran his finger along the shelf, and then snatched at a canvas. It was three feet high, and two feet wide. He took the canvas back to the easel and set it vertically on the crossbar. Connie left her place at the window and peeked curiously.

"It's orange!" she said.

Blake looked up, so distracted that the sound of her voice came as a surprise. "Huh?"

Connie pointed. "The canvas is orange."

"Yes," Blake said.

"But it's bright orange, Blake. Surely you can't paint on that!"

The canvas had been painted the same bright color as a ripe piece of the fruit.

Blake smiled indulgently. "Tips and techniques," he said vaguely. "Every one of my paintings was prepared the same way – under every canvas I showed you was this same shade of orange."

She didn't believe him and it wasn't until he selected several of the paintings she remembered so well and pointed to the edges of the gallery wrap where there was still orange residue that she finally lapsed into incredulous silence.

"White canvas is a common amateur mistake," Blake explained. "But for an artist who wants to paint realism, it just doesn't work. The finished painting always lacks something intangible."

"Which is?"

"Warmth," Blake said. "The warmth of the sun, the light. Everything in nature gives off warmth – even fence posts and innocuous inanimate objects. So I prepare the canvas and then lay down an undercoat of orange. Then, as I begin to work the painting, some of that orange color glows through the top layers, no matter how thickly the paint is applied. It just seems to radiate – and that's how I create depth and a sense of realism that maybe some other painters can't capture."

"But in a portrait?"

"It's just as important as it is in a seascape – maybe more," Blake said. "We'll find that out the day after tomorrow when we start work."

30.

The next morning Connie left early for Hoyt Harbor to collect the clothes and personal items she had left at the rental house, while Blake dusted Chloe's bedroom and changed the sheets.

He felt a burden lifted from his shoulders today; an unexpected sense of lightness that came from having shared the pain of Chloe's tragic death, and the shadow that incident had cast over his life. The grief never went away; the sorrow still seeped from him – and it always would – but now he sensed a glimpse of his old self emerging, rising up slowly to the surface from the darkness of despair.

He went to the bedroom window and stared out at the sweeping view of the beach. The morning was warm, the shadows across the sand shortening as the sun began to climb higher across the sky. Out on the ocean he could see the far off specks of fishing boats, bobbing like little corks on the swells, and closer to shore, the waves that curled before the beach were a translucent, vivid green.

It was a perfect summer's day – and with a shock, Blake realized suddenly how lonely he was.

It was Connie of course – she had infused herself into his life, coming bright and smiling like a high wind through a house and sweeping away the gloom and the sadness so that he missed her when she was gone. He stayed at the window but now the view became blank, replaced by a vision of her, and the poignant understanding in her face as she had wept for him the night before.

He was lonely, and he was alone. And he didn't want to feel like that any more. No matter how briefly Connie would be in his life, Blake decided it was at last time to make fresh memories – happy ones to fill the space in his heart he had given over to darkness.

He was also infected with an unexpected enthusiasm for painting once more. There was a tingle of anticipation in his fingers, and a feeling of daunting anxiety at the prospect of picking up his brushes and resurrecting the skills he had honed, directing them to a fresh challenge that was untainted by his memories. Never again would he paint the ocean, but now, at last, he would paint again. Maybe one last time – one last chance to create the perfect work, for always the looming threat of blindness hung over him.

He finished in Chloe's room, drew the window wide open and let the breeze off the ocean scour the walls of tears and sadness. The light spilled over the dark corners, chased away the ghosts of his regret, and then he closed the door quietly behind him.

Connie returned after lunch and came bursting and banging through the front door, calling out to him in gasps of laughter with a cardboard box in her arms. "I'm back!" she cried out. "Did you miss me?"

Her hair was awry, flicked across her face by the breeze and her cheeks were flushed pink. She dropped the box to the ground with a theatrical groan and stood back with her hands on her hips, breathing hard, her breasts beneath the tight cotton of her t-shirt rising and falling. She pouted her lips, blew the errant tendrils away from her face, and Blake couldn't help but smile.

"That's all of it?" he asked, glancing down at the box.

She nodded. "I'm the kind of girl who likes to travel light," she smiled playfully. "Everything else I own is in the trunk of the car."

Blake carried the box into the bedroom and stood back. Connie stepped across the threshold and cast her eyes around the room, taking it all in with a single glance. She went to the window as if drawn there, and stared out across the beach, standing on her tiptoes to see past the low shrubs so that Blake could not help but notice the cheeky clench of her bottom within the tightness of her jeans.

"The view is beautiful," Connie's voice brimmed with enthusiasm. "I don't think I've ever seen something quite so perfect."

"Nor me," Blake said with feeling.

31.

They spent the rest of the day cleaning out the studio, re-arranging furniture, and sweeping away great billowing clouds of dust so thick on the ground that when Thad Ryan arrived in the afternoon with the weekly delivery of groceries, he thought for a moment that the house had caught fire.

It was late in the afternoon when Blake stood back satisfied. His sleeves were rolled up high on his forearms and his shirt clung to his back with sweat. Connie was cleaning the window and she turned to him at last, exhausted, with dust on her face like a pale powdered mask.

"Enough," Blake decided and Connie threw down the cleaning rag into a bucket of dirty brown water.

They went down to the beach in a solemn procession at sunset and then Connie took charge of the kitchen with a subtle feminine propriety. She grilled steaks, gave Blake orders, and cooked ground beef for Ned. For the first time in as long as they could remember, both man and dog ate a meal that had not come from a can.

Connie and Blake were both exhausted, so that it was still early in the evening when Connie trudged wearily to bed. She fell onto the mattress with a great sigh of relief, but then sat up again abruptly when she heard Blake's uncertain footsteps outside the room, and then a polite gentle knock on the door.

"Yes?" She was naked. She drew the bed sheets beneath her armpits and clamped them there.

Blake pushed the door open a few inches.

"Is everything all right?" Connie asked in a husk.

Blake nodded. He glanced across the room as if maybe the words he wanted were written on the wall. "I just wanted you to know that I'm not crazy," he said softly. "In my head I know Chloe will never come back... but in my heart..."

Connie nodded. She felt his pain and his discomfort. She smiled in sympathy. "I understand, Blake. I truly do."

He nodded, but Connie sensed there was more he wanted to say and she fell silent to encourage him.

"I told you this place was like a prison to me. Remember?"

"Yes."

"It's because I can't leave," his voice began to choke and there was a lump of emotion lodged in his throat. "My heart won't let her go."

"That doesn't make you crazy," Connie whispered. "It makes you a good man."

32.

In the morning it was better. Gone was the melancholy of the evening, and in its place was an irrepressible sense of exhilaration, so unfamiliar that Blake struggled to recognize the feeling for what it was – excitement.

The studio door was open and he could see long shafts of sunlight spill into the hallway. He stood in the middle of the living room, his eyes drawn, but anxiety gnawing at his guts.

"Are you ready?" Connie seemed just as nervous.

He nodded, "It's now or never," he said prophetically.

Connie went to the studio window and tried to replicate the pose Blake had set her in when he had been planning the painting. She propped her hands on the window sill and saw her own face reflected in the glass. Over her shoulder she saw Blake rummaging through the wads of rags at the bottom of his painting box. He stood at last, clutching a camera.

"This morning I'll take all the reference photos," he explained as he quickly inspected the camera and cleaned the lens. "Then I'll project the final image, so I can begin painting this afternoon."

Connie looked intrigued. "Project?"

Blake nodded. "Digital projector," he explained. "It's a way to get a detailed image onto the canvas. Once I choose the photo I want to paint, the projector enlarges the image to the size of the canvas and I pencil in the outline. It gives me a highly detailed sketch that is the foundation for the painting."

"Isn't that considered cheating?" Connie asked naively. "I thought artists drew everything by hand."

Blake smiled. "That would be bad business," he said. "Especially for a realism artist. I want the most detailed image I can get before I start painting, so a projector just makes practical sense. Why spend days struggling with a sketch when people pay for my painting? They don't care about the drawing – they only care about the finished work, and using a projector saves time."

He fired off a dozen quick photos of Connie looking out through the window, testing the settings of the camera, and also getting a sense of the fall of light across her face. He was unhappy with the way she was positioned, but it was not until he scrolled back through those first images that he understood why. Looking at a scene was vastly different to looking at a photo. Now, as he stared through the digital display screen, he saw Connie framed and isolated, and recognized with an experienced eye why the images were not working.

He set the camera down and came to her. Connie was gripping the window sill as though she might fall. Then he had an inspired idea. He let it bloom in his mind for a moment, before dashing from the room. He came back a few moments later with one of the fresh roses Thad had brought with the weekly groceries. Without a word he handed the rose to Connie.

They were both aware of the subtle meaning, the significance of that moment, as though it was a deepening of the trust and understanding between them. Connie took the flower, realizing it was intensely important. She clutched the rose to her like it was precious.

"Take off your shirt," Blake said softly.

Connie was wearing a pale pink blouse. She unfastened the buttons one at a time, her fingers suddenly trembling. She could hear the pounding of blood at her temples, and her heart began to race. When at last the blouse gaped open, she slid it from her shoulders and stood, facing Blake.

The bra was white, delicately laced around the top of each cup in fine intricate whorls of pattern. Through the gauzy fabric Blake could see the dark shadows of her nipples, becoming hard. He nodded, said nothing. Connie picked up the rose again. Her eyes had become huge and soulful. She licked her lips.

Suddenly the world went very quiet. Outside the surf still pounded endlessly across the beach and the gulls still cried their lamenting calls, but in the studio, there was just the tense hum of deafening silence.

"Now hold the rose up to your face a little, as if you are inhaling the perfume," Blake's voice became very soft. They were so close he could feel the heat from her body, sense the quivering vibrations of her.

Connie's eyes were locked on Blake's. She couldn't breath. She lifted the rose slowly.

"Now turn your head a little to the side," Blake murmured.

He reached for the closest strap of her bra, and his fingers brushed against the flawless soft skin of

Connie's shoulder. He heard her gasp. His touch was soft, almost reverent, as though unwrapping some priceless gift. He drew the strap gently off her shoulder and reached around her to lower the other. His body brushed against hers and his senses became overwhelmed by the fragrance of her. He caught the scent in his breath and drank it down like elixir.

Connie felt the fine hairs along her forearms rise amongst a rash of goosebumps. She could feel tremors of fear and desire jangling along her spine. Blake eased the other strap from Connie's shoulder and then delicately brushed a tendril of hair from her cheek. His fingers lingered. Connie's flesh seemed to catch alight.

Blake took a step back, reached for the camera and snapped off several more shots. Connie watched him, her eyes liquid with simmering emotion.

"Look past my shoulder," Blake said quietly. Connie tore her gaze away, fixed her attention on a mark on the far wall. Blake took a dozen more photos, then came back to her again, standing so close that they seemed to share the same air.

Blake drew his fingers delicately once more across Connie's cheek and got lost in her eyes. He saw them fill with drowning desire, and knew that his own gaze was a mirror. Connie's lips were parted, pink and glossy. He heard her gasp a soft shuddering breath – and then he kissed her.

The warmth of her lips was a sensuous thrill that seemed to melt their mouths together. He slid an arm around her waist and she wrapped her hands about his neck, lacing her fingers into his hair, and lifting herself up onto her toes. Blake caressed the soft skin of her throat with his touch, and then gently cupped her chin within the palm of his hand. Her mouth against his was alive with her passion, her lips blooming open like the petals of a beautiful orchid as he drew her body close and she swayed against him until he could feel the urgent press of her breasts against his chest.

Blake heard singing in his ears, and then Connie whimpered softly. He brought his hand down across her chest and then placed it gently over her heart. He could feel the race of her pulse, the hectic pounding through the warmth of her skin. Connie nuzzled deeper into his arms until at last – at long last – they broke the kiss and came apart gasping and shaking, their eyes filled with a profound sense of shattering wonder.

33.

When Connie came back to the house in the afternoon there was high color in her cheeks and a luster to her skin from running with Ned along the beach. She was in a sparkling mood as she came down the hallway then quietly pushed open the door to the studio.

Blake was working at the easel, so absorbed that for long moments he did not realize she had returned. A spotlight clamped to the wooden frame above his head cast his features in stark relief. Connie saw the determined thrust of his chin, the hard shape of his jaw and the long line of his nose that met with the brow and darkened his eyes. His mouth was slack, the bottom lip thicker than the top one, his face made rugged by the shadow of stubble.

She stood uncertainly in the doorway until he seemed to sense her presence and looked up suddenly.

"Am I intruding?" Connie asked timidly.

"No," his expression changed in an instant, lighting up with pleasure. He smiled, and the warmth of it reached all the way to his eyes. "In fact I've been waiting for you."

He had been hunched on the chair. Now he stood up and stepped back from the canvas as though to invite her inspection. She came to him, standing deliberately close so that she could feel the press of his shoulder against her own, both of them delighting in the intimacy.

The canvas had been drawn up in great detail. On the paint table beside the chair was the reference photo, the size of an A4 sheet of paper that had been computer printed on glossy paper. Connie looked back at the canvas and studied the outline carefully. "So what do you paint first?" she asked.

"The eyes," Blake said without hesitation. "They're the essence of your personality. If I can't get those right, there's no point painting anything else because no matter how perfect everything else is rendered, it still won't be you."

"Is that normal?" Connie wondered.

"Painting the eyes of a portrait?"

"Yes – painting the most critical part of a canvas first. I thought with oil painting – because the oils take so long to dry – that you would have to work around the canvas in a way that didn't leave your hand smudging the areas you had completed."

"Well, painting the critical part of a seascape first isn't the way I ever approached a canvas," Blake admitted. "But then a seascape is a composite of so many elements – sky, surf, waves, rocks… they all have their place. A portrait, I think, is different. I can create a seascape and change elements. I can make the sky different, or paint the rocks in a shade different to the reference photo, and no one will ever know. I think a portrait requires more precision – it's not work for the incompetent or the fearful."

Connie seemed to understand Blake's explanation, but she lingered by the easel just to be near him for a few moments longer. The moment he kissed her had haunted her ever since. She still felt little flutters of her heart, like lingering tremors that follow a quake.

His fingers brushed against hers. She seized his hand and squeezed tight. "I have faith in you," she smiled, and then began plucking at the buttons of her blouse.

Connie went to the window, carefully picked up the rose, and stood in position. The light was different now – the sun had long passed over the house and was slowly setting in the west. She took a deep breath to compose herself, then stood perfectly still.

Blake went across to the counter. There was an old paint-spattered radio on a shelf. He found a station playing classic rock and turned up the music.

"I'll be doing some color mixing exercises for a while," he explained. "I've never spent any time working with skin tones before – my palette has always been filled with cool colors. So feel free to move around if you like until I can get a handle on shades and shadows. Once I have the colors right I'll set that all aside and begin on your eyes."

Blake worked over the palette like an alchemist for an hour, squeezing thick swirls of paint from their tubes, mixing, and then dabbing little touches of the colors directly onto the photograph for comparison. As he worked, Connie gazed out of the window, humming contentedly along to the tunes until he was at last ready for her.

From amidst the rags on his paint table, Blake produced a pair of glasses. The frames were thick and black – the kind of spectacles worn by fashionable movie stars, or struggling authors. He set them on the end of his nose and came to stand close to Connie.

"Look at me," he said softly.

She swung her eyes to his, lifted her face and gazed at him, her expression so open that he could see the secrets of her soul.

"You have the most beautiful eyes," he breathed, leaning close enough to kiss her again. "They're brown, flecked with tawny gold."

He went back to the canvas then and snatched up the reference photo, studying it with all his attention. At last he grunted, selected a fine-pointed brush with bristles that were soft in his fingers, and began to melt paint onto the canvas.

Blake worked for three hours, absorbed in the challenge of subtly blending shades within the irises, so that time and space seemed to dissolve around him. At last when he looked up, the light through the window was no more than a soft memory of the day that had passed them by. He stood with a stiff groan and arched his aching back.

"I'm out of condition," he grunted with a regrettable shake of his head.

Connie was impatient. "Can I see?"

She went to the canvas and stared at the eerie image – a pair of isolated eyes, painted to stunning completion, so that they looked as though they had been cut carefully from a photo and fixed to the canvas. She peered close, utterly fascinated, and then frowned. "Are the whites of my eyes really that... that grey-blue color?" there was an edge like horrified panic in her voice.

Blake laughed, and realized how much he enjoyed the sound of it in his own ears. "It's relative,

I assure you," he grinned. "You're seeing that color without any reference. When we look at color, our vision draws in all the surrounding shades and sort of blends them together – one tone affects those around it. So if you look at a shade of red in isolation, and then alongside, say blue, the red shade will appear different, even though it is exactly the same color."

"Is that what's happening here?" she pointed at the painting.

Blake nodded. "You're seeing the whites of your eyes without any color around them. Once I get the skin tones painted in, it will make more sense."

"And I have no eyelashes?"

"Not yet," Blake explained. "That's the type of fine detail added at the end of the painting when the flesh around your cheeks and brow are dry."

Connie nodded thoughtfully and then once again looked up into his face as if now seeking some kind of assurance. "Are you happy with it?" she asked, because it was the most important question of all – the only one that mattered to her right then.

Blake considered the question gravely, narrowing his eyes and inspecting the afternoon's work one last time with a critical glare. "Yes," he said at last.

34.

The sunset was masked by dark boiling clouds that came in from the ocean, so that night fell early and thunder rumbled across the sky. A howling wind clawed along the exposed beach, bending the long grasses and shredding the leaves from the trees. Blake stood on the shore with his shirt flattened against his chest and the sand blasting like a thousand tiny needles against his exposed skin. He set the rose into the surf and came away from the churning waterline with the gusting gale pressing like a hand in the middle of his back. A flash of lightning tore the sky apart so that for a split-second he could see the silhouette of Connie and Ned, close together, waiting for him.

They went up through the narrow trail side by side and reached the shelter of the porch before the first drops of rain fell.

"This is just the start of what's about to come. It will get worse," Blake said ominously.

A jagged blue fork of lighting shredded the night, seeming to touch the far horizon, and beside him Blake felt Connie tremble with the sudden cold. He put his arm around her and they went inside, closing windows throughout the house as the rain became a constant drumming.

For hours the storm seemed to ebb and flow, crashing down with furious violence and then relenting to an eerie stillness, before coming back once more, with a roar like a wounded beast. Connie fried eggs in the kitchen, glancing out through the window as wind-whipped debris was dashed against the house and the rain at the glass sounded like flung gravel.

At nine o'clock, Ned rose from his bed and went out onto the porch, his eternal vigil begun for the night. Connie glimpsed him through the door, the big dog as docile and unmoving as a sphinx.

"Shouldn't you call him inside," Connie fretted. She went to a window and pressed her nose to the glass, watching the Great Dane as rain poured from the flooded guttering and spattered the dog until he was soaked and shivering.

"He won't move," Blake said simply and then felt compelled to explain to take the harshness from his words. "This isn't the first storm we've had here, Connie. The dog is stubborn. His loyalty won't allow him to forsake Chloe, not even on a night like this."

He brought the old radio from the studio and they turned the music up to drown out the drumming roar of the rain, then sat on the couch together, discovering the novelty of their closeness. Connie's hands rested in her lap, Blake's arm relaxed around her shoulder. She was leaning against him, her cheek pressed to his chest, lulled by the steady sound of his breathing, while outside the world seemed torn apart by the terrible fury of nature.

An old rock song came on the radio and impulsively Connie leaped to her feet. Uninhibited, she began moving to the beat, swinging her hips and swishing the long mane of her hair with her eyes closed, as though she could feel the rhythm of the music flow through her body. Blake watched with dignified restraint, rejecting her invitations to join her, delighting in the liquid way her body

186

moved and the free-spirited joy that showed in the smile on her face.

By the time the song ended, the storm seemed once again to have relented. The rain became steady and the wind across the beach faded to an undulating moan. Suddenly the music sounded painfully loud. Blake came up from the sofa, turned the radio off, and took Connie's wrist. He pulled her close so that she gasped in surprise.

For an instant they stared into each other's eyes, and then they kissed again.

Connie's arms went around Blake and she ran her splayed fingers up his back. Blake cupped Connie's face within the palms of his hands and felt the tantalizing flicker of her tongue across his lips. Their mouths opened and Connie whimpered deep in her throat. She dug her clawed nails into the broad of Blake's shoulders like a cat responding to a caress.

"I want you," Blake murmured, his mouth sliding down her throat so that she could feel the delicious rasp of his stubbled chin and cheeks against the soft exposed skin. She arched her spine with a voluptuous shudder, bent backwards by the sudden intensity of his desire, and she was panting with her own desperate need. Her eyes were closed, her lips parted. She gasped when Blake's fiery kisses hunted down to the deep V of her collar. She felt his hands everywhere, exploring the curve of her breasts and the narrowness of her waist – and she wanted more.

Connie tore her eyes open, planted a hand in the middle of Blake's chest. Over his shoulder she could see the long corridor leading to the bedroom.

"I want you too," she groaned with a sound of torn frustration. "But not here, Blake. Not yet."

He sobered suddenly, the mist clearing from his eyes. They were both still panting, but his arms about her slackened and Connie kissed him again in reassurance.

"When the house is a little less sad, I promise," she whispered, her voice still hoarse and shaking with lust. "I just want our first time to be a new moment, not have the happiness of it tinged by the shreds of your sadness. Not the first time..."

He frowned, yet seemed to understand. Light and laughter were coming back into the house, yet still there were dark unfiltered corners. He set his jaw determinedly.

"I want you," he said again.

"And I want you," Connie whispered desperately. "But..."

He covered her mouth with a kiss so fierce and fiery that Connie felt her bones go soft, her body melt. The scorch of his lips seemed infused with an intensity that stole her breath away. Then, quite suddenly, Blake scooped her up in his arms and held her across his chest. Connie threw her hands around his neck, torn between her desire and her willingness to please him.

"Blake –"

He covered her mouth again, stifling her protest, until she fell silent into breathless pants. "Woman, you talk too much."

Blake went to the door with Connie in his arms, swung it open with his foot and walked out into the storm-torn night. Ned was on the porch. He did not move. Blake went down the steps and strode broad-shouldered towards the beach. Lightning flashed again, brightening the shore with a flicker of dazzling glow so he could see the narrow path and the outlines of the trees.

Drizzle spattered their shoulders, then thunder rumbled and rolled across the sky. The heavens opened, soaking them so that their clothes clung drenched to their bodies and rain streamed from their faces.

Blake carried Connie down to the beach. The sand was hard under his feet. The wind had died to a whisper and in the darkness he could hear the pounding rumble of the waves as they burst upon the shore. The ground seemed to hum with the vibration of the surf's fury.

Blake peeled off his sodden shirt and laid it on the ground. Connie sank to the sand and Blake stood over her for an instant, bare-chested. He lifted his face to the stormy sky and let the rain wash over his face and chest, and Connie caught her breath. He looked like a Norse god, risen from the sea, born of the storm. His body was glistening as if oiled, the muscles in his shoulders and arms standing in proud relief while the clouds swirled about him and the sky was lit with its awesome wrath.

He dropped into the sand beside her and suddenly she was alive and passionate within the strong embrace of his arms. He tore at her blouse and Connie encouraged him with feverish pants of breath. She arched her back, lifted her mouth up to his, and pulled him down onto her with a kiss that seemed filled with a passion and emotion that had been wrenched from her very soul.

They made love in the crashing tempest, and each erotic moment seemed lit by a flash of lightning that seared the images forever into Blake's mind. He saw the curve of Connie's throat, her head thrown back and her eyes screwed tightly shut with delight. He saw the sway of her breasts and the delicate hardened nubs of her nipples as the downpour spilled in glistening rivulets across her undulating body. He saw the wanting in her eyes, burning as fierce as his own – and then he felt the urgency in her, and the welcoming warmth of her when at last there was nothing between them. She lunged with her hips to meet him as they rocked together in a timeless rhythm that was as old as the crashing sea, as urgent as the beat of the universe.

The rain drummed on Blake's back, and the storm roared its fury across the sky until at last the night began to clear and the first stars hung bright overhead. Their cries lapped and eddied together, rising and falling, until the thunder crashed one final rumbling time, so loud as to cover their strangled groans of ragged release.

For long moments afterwards they lay still under the stars. Connie turned her face slowly to Blake's and he could feel the lingering shudders of her breath on his cheek. He kissed her tenderly, and she curled up in his arms. He kneaded her back with strong fingers and then she rolled away again, one hand thrown languidly across her naked belly. She had never felt such intensity of emotion before and she lay there floating dreamily in astonishment and wonder. She could still feel the press of his body, her flesh still smoldered from the flames of his touch and not even the spattering rain could extinguish the burn. She closed her eyes, savoring the sensations as though it were a moment to be cherished.

Blake propped himself up onto one elbow and stared at Connie with dark contemplative eyes.

She sensed the heat of his gaze and turned her eyes toward him. She tried to smile, but her lips were trembling and shaky. "What do you see?" she asked softly, her voice a low self-conscious husk.

"I see beauty," Blake's voice was raw. He traced his finger delicately along her eyebrow. "The most beautiful woman I have ever laid eyes on."

She smiled but it was a shy little thing that she could not hold on her lips because she did not believe him. She glanced away, but he cupped her cheek in his palm and turned her face back.

"I have spent endless hours studying your face and taking photos of you," Blake said solemnly "and yet I don't think I ever saw you quite as clearly, or as perfectly as I see you right now."

35.

For the next fourteen days Blake worked on the portrait and each brush stroke bled with his passion and skill. Slowly the image began to take form and substance before his eyes, and after the first few days of methodical plodding, his skills came back, honed and sharp, and the deftness of his touch returned. He began covering the canvas after each session in the studio, sensing the magic of emotion that seemed to infuse the work, and Connie pouted and pleaded, then gave up with a petulant huff, accepting that she would not see the painting again until it was complete.

He worked at the easel during the day, when the sun was bright and warm through the window, and then in the afternoon Connie would coax him from the studio, out into the afternoon. They ran on the beach, splashing in the surf, and then fell to the hot sand gasping and laughing with Ned circling, happy to share in their joy.

They explored the rocky cliffs at both ends of the beach, scrambling over the craggy outcrops until Connie's skin colored to honey and the soft freckles across her nose glowed like flakes of gold.

One afternoon they found a secluded rock pool with the water as deep as their waists, and they waded into the sun-warmed ripples and embraced beneath the afternoon sky. Connie peeled off her t-shirt and the soft skin of her breasts, untouched by the sun, was a stark contrast to the polished amber of the rest of her body. Blake bowed his head to her nipple and she guided him down with her hands, a husky moan of contentment humming in her throat. He wrapped his arms around her and traced his fingertips down the arch of her spine, his touch fluttering at first and then bolder. Connie felt her legs tremble and her whole body began to undulate and thrust against him.

They made love in the long grass of the headland and then lay in the shade when the sun became too hot, lazy and loving and watching on in idyllic bliss while the sunshine glinted the horizon line into a string of sparkling diamonds.

On another day they went walking with a picnic basket into the dense pine forest that backed onto the house, and Blake led Connie to a secluded glade. The sun sprinkled light though the canopy of the trees and the air was thick and humid. Faint on the air they could hear the distant drum of the ocean, but it seemed and sounded a million miles away.

Blake spread a blanket and Connie laid out the food and drink between then. Blake plucked at a long finger of grass and tickled her nose. Connie swatted at his hand and they went tumbling over together in a shriek of outrageous laughter as he pulled her off balance.

Afterwards, when they were naked on the blanket, Connie lay on her side, studying Blake's face with frank scrutiny while he stared lazily up into the sky as it began to fill with white clouds.

"I like your lips," Connie said seriously, tracing the outline of them with the curious tip of her finger. "They're good for kissing."

Blake suppressed a smile. Her touch was a tickle at the corner of his mouth and he twitched his nose. "I like your lips too," he said.

She ignored him. One of her hands was flat on his chest. With the other she drew a line along his nose, feeling the ridges and little bumps, each one an ancient story.

"Was your nose ever broken?" she asked.

"Once, playing football," he said.

She continued exploring. There was an old scar on his chin, and another on his chest, almost hidden in the whorls of dark hair there. She touched it, felt the raised little ridge, and then moved her hand inexorably lower, becoming bolder.

"I like your mind," she said at last.

Blake flicked her a curious glance. He wedged an arm under his head. "My mind?"

"You're quite brilliant," she said seriously. "Your art – the way you see things, and then the way you go about painting."

Blake gave a dismissive grunt. "Ninety percent of my painting was a result of simple hard work," he said. "It wasn't brilliance, it was persistence. I was just too stupid to give up. I didn't invent anything new, Connie. I just stumbled on techniques by accident."

She sat up and scowled at him. "Then how do you explain the portrait?" she challenged. "The techniques must be totally different to painting a seascape, and yet I know your new painting is amazing. I just know it."

He taunted her. "How do you know that? Have you peeked? Have you crept into the studio and seen it when I wasn't around?"

She shook her head. "I just know," she said. "Otherwise you would let me see it."

"Well maybe I am hiding it from you because it is awful?"

Her fingers had crawled towards his abdomen. She gripped at him suddenly and he yelped in alarm. Connie's face was a fiendish giggle of mischief. "Tell me the truth," her voice was silken with soft playful menace. "Is it wonderful?"

"I haven't ruined it yet," Blake countered.

Connie squeezed gently and Blake let out a nervous laugh. "Okay! It's good," he surrendered. "It's very good."

Connie smiled with triumph. Suddenly Blake was hot and hard in her hand. She made her eyes wide and artless, and caught her breath. "Goodness," she murmured. "Well we can't let *that* go to waste!"

At the end of the first week Connie drove into Hoyt Harbor and spent the day shopping. She bought herself a new cell phone, and called Jean with the new number, then contacted the nursing home with the same information.

When she came back in the afternoon, Blake was finishing in the studio. The air in the room was heavy with the odor of turpentine. He washed his brushes, wiped them carefully dry, and then met Connie on the porch steps. She was brimming with excitement, her eyes alive and dancing. She threw herself into his arms, her laughter like the tinkle of a bell.

"I think I've found the perfect place for a studio," she bubbled, gripping at his arms and skipping from one foot to the other. "It's a shop on the main street of Hoyt Harbor, just a few doors down from the grocery store. There was a real estate office there, but they are closing down – Blake it would be perfect, absolutely perfect," the words came in an uninterrupted rush without breath or pause.

She dragged him by the hand, down into the sand and drew a map with the end of a stick, showing him the layout of the office and outlining her plans. Blake watched her, became infected by her enthusiasm, and pored over the crude drawing. He sat back at last and rubbed his chin thoughtfully.

"Is it going to be big enough?"

Connie nodded, certain. "I paced it out," she explained. "The office is one long narrow space, with a separate corner office. That would be the storage area," she proposed. "But the walls in the main room would allow me to hang forty – maybe forty-five good-sized canvases. No trouble."

"What about window frontage?"

"There is some," Connie said. "The realtor that is in the premises has a display of houses available. The window isn't wide, but it reaches from the floor to the ceiling. Beside it is a door into the shop."

Blake's brow was still furrowed. "What about lighting?"

"It's good," Connie said. "But I would probably need to improve it."

Blake sat back on his haunches. Connie was gazing at him, yearning silently for his approval. She stared at him with big wide eyes.

"What about the rent?"

She told him and he was surprised. It was affordable.

"They need a tenant as soon as possible. The tourist season is almost over and I guess the landlord knows that once the vacationers go, his chances of filling the shop before next season are slim."

"When would you open?"

Connie shrugged. She stared down into the sand for a silent moment, her lips pursed, trying to calculate the time she would need to have lighting fitted and the walls repainted. "Maybe in a month or two?" it was more of a question than an answer.

"And what would you open with?"

She blushed coyly. "Your paintings – if you will still let me show them. I thought I could hold an opening night, invite the mayor and local dignitaries, as well as some of the art media. It would be a big deal in the art world – not the gallery, but a showing of your long-lost works. It could launch the gallery, give me a profile, and help me to attract other big-name artists."

Blake arched his eyebrows, probing her plan, getting a sense of her commitment. "So you will be a high-end gallery?"

"Yes," Connie said adamantly. "There is already the gallery on the foreshore that exhibits local art for tourists. I am thinking much grander. I want the big name artists to consign me pieces."

"And you think you can attract the sort of money that invests in high-end art all the way to Hoyt Harbor?"

"They will come for you, Blake. They will come from all around the world to see your paintings," Connie said earnestly. "I am counting on them coming back when I have other artists to show them. And if not, I can always deal through the internet."

Blake got slowly to his feet. The sun was lowering and the sky was beginning to tint in the hues of a glorious sunset. "Well it sounds as though you have it all thought out," he said. "I don't see what's stopping you."

She came to him and hugged him fiercely. "So you will still allow me to show your paintings?"

"Yes," he smiled into her big bright eyes.

"And the new one? The portrait?"

"That's up to you," he said. "I plan on giving it to you as a gift when it's finished. You can do with it what you want. Show it, sell it..."

"Oh, no," Connie said gravely. "I would never sell it. It's our painting, Blake. A painted memory of the happiest days of my life."

To celebrate, they carried a folding table down to the beach that night and ate grilled steaks on the shore, watching the moon as it seemed to rise up from out of the ocean, and marveling at the glittering brightness of the stars. The sea was calm, the waves whispering up onto the sand. Blake fetched a blanket from the house and they lay on the beach talking until midnight when at last the mist came roiling off the ocean and turned the world pearlescent grey.

The following morning Connie phoned the landlord, and the Connie Dixon Gallery of Fine Art was born.

36.

Just as the days were filled with work, and the afternoons given over to the sun and the sand, so the nights were reserved for their loving.

Connie came to Blake's bed every evening and they devoured each other in the erotic intensity of lovemaking. Each time together seemed more poignant, more touching so that no two nights were the same. They learned the secret pleasures of each other's bodies, the subtle caresses and touches that aroused, and discovered their appetites were equally unquenchable – they could not get enough of each other.

When Connie came to him quietly one night during the second week, she stood in the open doorway for long moments with the light from the hallway behind her back. She was naked, and she called out to him quietly in the darkened room.

"Yes," he husked.

She glided across the floor, an ethereal figure of femininity, and climbed beneath the sheets beside him. Her body was warm and her fingers alive with new enthusiasm. She rolled atop him and straddled his hips. She kissed him tenderly. He reached up with his hand and brushed the fall of her hair from her face – and realized with a shock that she had been weeping.

"What's wrong?" he asked

She sniffed, and then laughed at herself. "I'm happy," she said.

She kissed him again, more passionate than before, and they became entangled within each other's arms. Outside the night was still and quiet, but on the big bed their lovemaking was a fresh storm of passion until they lay back spent and exhausted, as though they had plumbed the very depths of human emotion.

Much later, when they were still and quiet, their breathing just a whisper, Connie rose, but Blake flung an arm around her waist to stop her.

"No more," he said. "No more going back to another room. Stay here with me from now on."

37.

Blake leaned in close, fixed his gaze with infinite concentration, and then dabbed at the canvas with the tip of a fine-pointed brush. His hand was steady, and every minute stroke was a painstaking exercise in control as he spread oil paint across the small piece of canvas. At last he sat back, widened his eyes, and then blinked. He felt himself release a breath he hadn't realized he had been holding.

He turned to the palette, loaded the small brush with a mix of paynes grey and crimson, and set it alongside the pure color beside it – working in a small section of the painting no larger than his thumb. When the dark shade was spread evenly, he snatched up a badger brush and fanned out the bristles with the tips of his fingers until the sable was soft.

"What kind of a brush is that?" Connie asked from where she stood by the window.

"Badger brush," Blake grunted.

"What's it for?" She was glum, peering out through the glass listlessly for most of the day, distracted by a swirl of fears that tumbled in her mind. The painting was almost complete, and with it was ending Blake's reason for needing her here. For two weeks she had closed her mind to the realization that their time was limited. Now it would soon be a reality, and that inevitable certainty filled her with worry.

"It's for blending colors together," Blake said. He had sensed her mood, but been preoccupied with the canvas. "It's like an old fashioned version of an airbrush that artists use these days," he went on as he worked the paint with deft flicks of his wrist until the two colors seemed to magically melt together to become the petal of the rose.

He threw the brush down, stood stiffly and hung his neck to the side to loosen knotted muscles.

"Now," he stepped away from the easel. "Would you mind telling me what your problem is?"

"Problem?"

He nodded. "You've been downcast all day, waiting for me to notice. Something is bothering you. What is it?"

Connie drooped her shoulders, seemed to wilt tragically. She gave a heavy theatrical sigh and shook her head. "Nothing."

Blake lifted her chin with the tips of his fingers so he could see into her eyes. She was pouting like a child and he almost laughed. He repeated the question patiently.

"The painting is almost finished," Connie said.

"Yes."

She fell silent as though Blake should surely understand.

"And...?"

Connie made a sad little face. "And then you won't need me here any more."

Blake nodded. "Is that what this is about?"

"Yes."

He stood back, folded his arms, his expression dire and serious. "What about the exhibition you are planning for your new gallery?"

Connie looked up suddenly. "What about it?"

Blake shrugged as though it should be obvious. "Well won't you need to catalogue all my old seascape paintings, then photograph them, and then write detailed descriptions and produce a brochure?"

Connie was startled. "Yes..."

"And won't you need constant access to the paintings to do all that work?"

"Yes," she said with dawning realization.

"And do you really want to drive to and from Hoyt Harbor every day to do that?"

She shook her head now. She was smiling, the warmth of it spreading like a glorious sunrise across her face. "That would be horrible."

Blake nodded, then leaned forward and kissed her on the tip of her nose. "Then it's settled. Now can I get back to work?"

He stared at the petal of the rose with a critical eye, and decided that to do any more would risk muddying the colors and losing the vibrancy of their pigments. He set the badger brush aside, but stayed standing for another long moment, squinting his eyes and inclining his head to one side as if to see the work from a fresh angle. He was almost done for the day.

He went back to the chair and worked for another thirty minutes, massaging wet oil paint until he had shape and shadow. He added a touch of white to the crimson and then worked with the infinite precision of a jeweler until the missing element – shine – seemed to give the petal an impossible third dimension.

Blake tossed the brush aside and straightened his back. He heard tiny bones crack. He wiped his hands on a scrap of cloth, and then smeared the rest of the paint from his fingertips with turpentine.

A puzzling sound made him look up curiously. It was muffled through walls and for an instant he didn't recognize it. Connie did.

"My phone!" she said, and went running from the room.

38.

Connie ran into the living room, rummaged around in her purse and snatched up the phone before the call went to voice mail. She was breathing hard, filled with an unaccountable dread. She expected to hear the dispassionate voice of the nursing home director, preparing her for news about her mother.

"Hello?" she said breathless.

"Hello, darling," Duncan Cartwright's voice seemed to drip with sarcasm. Connie's hand clutched at her throat, her fingers feathered and trembling.

"Duncan?" Connie hissed. She was incredulous. She felt icy tentacles of foreboding wrap around her heart, as if the misery of her past had suddenly reappeared like a dark cloud on the horizon. "How did you get this number?"

"Well that took some artful deception," he admitted. His voice was malicious with his triumph. "Let's just say the people at your mother's nursing home are a little too gullible. You really should talk to them, you know." He was smiling, she could hear it in his voice and it sickened her.

"What do you want?" She cast a furtive glance back down the hallway and could see Blake's shadow moving on the wall as he worked in the studio. She went into the kitchen and found a corner at the table.

"I wanted to talk to you about your paintings, darling," Duncan seemed unaffected by the harsh tone of Connie's voice. "You left some of your early work here in the gallery's basement. It's all rubbish of course, and I have thrown out the one you gave to me. Remember that one – some childish little mess that you thought made a handsome birthday gift." There was a brief pause and then his voice changed in an instant. "I want them gone," he growled. "Or else I'll burn them."

Connie stared vacantly at the far wall. She had given Duncan one of her early paintings, when he had been so encouraging about her work. She had forgotten about them until now. She wanted them back, not because they had value, but because they were like landmarks along her life journey.

"Will you come and get your painting?" Duncan asked again.

"Yes, I'll get the painting."

"And the rest of this vile trash?"

She ignored the barb. "Yes," Connie whispered. "I will, Duncan. I will get them all. I already told you I would."

"When?"

"Soon!" She was thinking furiously, wondering how quickly she could arrange for a courier to collect the work from New York and have it delivered. Duncan spoke across the silence.

"I miss you in my bed," he taunted her. "You were so good, baby, and I know it was good for you too – the way you used to moan and beg me for more."

"No," Connie said with a sneer. "I did it because I had to, not out of love or passion, Duncan. Never. I just went through the motions to survive – and every single time I was revolted."

She hung up the phone and threw it across the table.

* * *

Blake heard Connie's footsteps fade down the long hallway and then the trilling sound of her phone abruptly stopped. He turned his attention once more to the painting. He grunted with a grudging satisfaction and pride. The portrait was finished, and even he had to admit that it was beautiful.

The painting had been rendered with all of his dedication and talent. Connie's face was an expression of longing – as though some secret sadness welled behind her eyes, sparked perhaps by the fragrance of the rose she held. The detail was exquisite. The light across her face and arms was so real it seemed as though the canvas had been backlit – a painting made translucent and alive by his skill.

He leaned over the bottom of the canvas, signed his name with a flourish, and left the room. Tomorrow morning he would show Connie.

He wandered down the long hall and heard Connie still talking on the phone, her tone harsh and almost belligerent. Blake stopped, stunned, then felt an icy chill run through his blood. He guessed she was in the kitchen, her voice a hoarse whisper as though the conversation was secret. He moved quietly to the end of the hallway and caught her reflection in one of the windows.

Connie was hunched over the kitchen table. Her hand seemed to be cupped around the phone. She was staring vacantly at a wall, her face twisted in an angry frown. Then suddenly he heard her voice become strident, as though incensed.

"Yes, I'll get the painting." She hissed.

Blake's expression became monstrous with betrayal. He felt his heart drop and everything around him began to swirl.

"Yes," Connie hissed again. *"I will, Duncan. I will get them all. I already told you I would."*

Blake felt himself begin to shake.

Connie said abruptly, *"Soon!"*

And then the anger came upon him, like a black unholy rage. He felt his blood begin to boil, and at the same time a wrenching pain like despair pierced his heart so that he almost folded over and clutched at his chest. He began to shake his head in slow disbelief.

"No," Connie said into the phone, her tone now derisive and withering. *"I did it because I had to, not out of love or passion, Duncan. I just went through the motions to survive – and every single time I was revolted."*

She hung up the phone, threw it down on the table as though it was diseased. Then she buried her hands in her face and began to sob softly.

Blake came around the corner. His eyes were dark and dead, his face filled with loathing. He glared across the kitchen to where Connie sat with his jaws clenched.

"You played me for a fool," he said, and then stalked back down the hall towards the studio.

39.

Blake was staring out through the studio window when Connie came running into the room. She could see the bristling tension in the rigid set of his shoulders, the ragged draw of each breath, and the bunched knuckles of his fists, heavy at his side like hammers.

Connie paused, suddenly afraid. Her eyes were red, her face stricken with distress. She was shaking her head in numb heartbroken agony. Shock and fear churned in her stomach.

"Blake?" she tried to reach out to him with an aching plea in her voice. "I don't know how much you overheard of that phone call, but please believe me when I tell you it's not what you think."

Blake wheeled round, his mouth twisted in bitterness and excruciating pain. His eyes were black as coal. The lines of his face seemed more deeply etched. The expression on his face was so tortured that Connie's breath locked in her throat.

"You betrayed me," he seethed.

Connie shook her head. "No," she said softly.

He laughed, but it was a hollow incredulous sound. "You wanted my paintings," he shook his head, for he could not believe how gullible he had been. "And I should have known. I should have realized this whole time you were manipulating me – playing me so you could get your hands on the canvases. I don't know who you're working with, and I don't care. I just can't believe you would..." the cruel words choked off, and he stared at her with nothing but contempt in his eyes.

For a long time Blake fell ominously silent, then at last the anger seemed to come boiling back upon him. He flung his arms wide, encompassing the room in a careless gesture. "Take them," he growled. "Take them all – and while you're at it..." he dug his hands deep into the pockets of his jeans and turned them out so she could see a few loose coins. "You might as well take these too." He tossed the money down on the floor.

Connie was crying miserably, shaking her head in slow mute denial.

"That's all I've got," Blake sneered derisively at her. "Now you have everything... including the only two things I ever clung to – that I ever held precious," he extended his palms towards Connie so that each of them was flat. "My trust, and my secrets."

Suddenly he slammed his hands tight into fists, as though the things they held had been crushed and destroyed. "I hope you're happy."

Connie felt herself sway with nausea. The knot of excruciating agony that burned in her chest was choking her.

"Blake!" She cried out his name suddenly as though it had been gasped with her last breath. She went to him and tried fiercely to bury herself within his arms. She pressed her cheek against his chest, flattened her body against him with desperation. She was sobbing uncontrollably. She felt the world reeling around her and for startled, appalling seconds, Blake did not move.

"Blake, you don't understand," Connie wept against him. "It's not what you think. I swear it to you."

He seized her shoulders and held her away from him. He was shaking with rage and Connie seemed to sway on her feet. "Get away from me," the words seemed to scald his tongue. "Take the paintings and get out of this house, and out of my life, before I –"

He let Connie go. There were angry red marks high on her arms from the clench of his fingers. Her face had drained of all color and she was trembling. Her cheeks were slick with tears, her mouth wide open and her face filled with horror. She stared at him, sickened and shaken.

"Blake no!" she cried out. "Don't say that," she sobbed. "At least let me explain."

"Explain?" he snarled, his voice like a whiplash. "There's nothing to explain, Connie. I heard every word you said about getting the painting, getting them all..." his voice lowered and became filled with acid revulsion, "and I heard what you said about us – about what you had to endure to get them."

He spun away, glaring back out through the window. He could see his own reflection in the glass – see the clutch of raw pain in his face and the despair in his eyes. He was shaking with rage and hurt, like a wounded beast that had been shot through the heart and was bleeding to death.

He heard Connie's shuffled leaden footsteps, slowly retreating towards the door of the studio. He didn't turn. He closed his eyes and prayed that she would go, just leave him alone to drift into his own private sorrow so he could ride the waves of betrayal that washed over him. He felt numb, bereft. At last he heard the door quietly close. He took a deep shuddering breath and turned around, empty and broken.

Connie was still in the room. She was standing with her back against the door, as if she needed its support to stay on her feet. Her head was lowered, her shoulders slumped in capitulation. Her hair hung down over her face and Blake could hear her sobbing softly, each gasp of breath wracked with her own pain.

"That phone call was from a man named Duncan Cartwright," Connie whispered, as though she were speaking to the floor. "He was my boss at the gallery where I worked," she lifted her head slowly and the veil of dark hair fell away from her eyes so that Blake could see the hurt of her own memories, "and for four years he was also using me for sex."

Suddenly the room went very quiet. Blake could hear the rasp of his own breathing, and feel the throb of pulse at his temples. He stared across the space of the room at Connie but did not move. He felt the rigid expression on his face begin to crack and crumble. His hateful expression wavered slightly.

"When I left home and moved to New York it was because I wanted to be an artist," Connie said. "I had no money, but I had a desperate dream to paint. Duncan discovered me. He groomed me," she said the words without thinking, then realized how true they were. "He told me I had talent, and encouraged me to keep painting. He paid my bills until I was in debt to him, and then he started seeking repayment... with sex," Connie said. Shame was swirling in her eyes, but she lifted her chin so that Blake could see the honesty of her words. Her bottom lip was trembling, her face a tear-slicked mask of tragedy as she was forced to cast her mind back over the nightmares that she had tried so hard to forget.

"He would come to my apartment, and use me. I had no choice..." she said softly, and then admonished herself. A small choke of self-pity constricted in the back of her throat. "I was old enough to know better, but desperate enough to do whatever it took to fulfill my dream."

Connie had her hands clasped in front of her. She wrung them together as though the pain of the words had become unbearable. "Then he took my dream away from me. He had promised me exhibitions, but he never delivered. One day I woke up and realized that I was too deep in debt to escape, and that Duncan owned me. He had taken my dream and trapped me within it. When he said I wasn't good enough to exhibit, he offered me work as a dealer for the gallery."

Connie shrugged. She was looking into Blake's face, but seeing another time. Her voice had become small and withdrawn. "I had no choice," she said with a sick little slide of regret and bitterness. "I was too deeply in his debt. He was paying for my apartment and helping with payments to keep my mother in a nursing home. He had bought me as his whore, and I never really realized it until I was in too deep to ever escape."

Blake felt some of the tension go from his body. His hands relaxed. He was watching Connie, and some of the anger began to melt from his gaze. He felt himself frown in a flicker of sympathy.

"I told you I was in trouble," Connie admitted. "I used the small painting I bought from Warren Ryan to pay Duncan back and free myself."

"That doesn't explain the phone call," Blake's voice was gruff but had lost its sting. "What you said on the phone. What I heard you tell him about the paintings... about us..."

Connie shook her head with sudden vehemence. She saw the waver of doubt in Blake's eyes and her expression became imploring. "That call wasn't about your paintings, and it wasn't about us," Connie said passionately. "I gave Duncan a painting two years ago for his birthday. That call was about my old pieces of art he still has stored at the gallery. He wants them gone, or he is going to burn them."

"And us?"

She became suddenly sad, as though all she had confessed had left her devastated. Her eyes were like empty sockets. "He asked me whether I missed him. He taunted me about the sex, the way he had wanted me to act in his bed."

Blake took a deep breath and closed his eyes. He felt a wave of light-headed relief wash over him. She had not betrayed him. Nothing else mattered.

She had not betrayed him.

"I see," he said thickly. "Why didn't you tell me this?"

"Because I thought it was the past," Connie said earnestly. "When I went back to New York and gave Duncan the painting, I thought he was out of my life forever. It was a time I am not proud of, Blake. Something that I wanted to bury and forget.

I didn't call him – somehow he got my new number from the nursing home."

There was a long silence. They stared at each other across the room. The tension had gone, replaced by relief, sadness, and tenuous uncertainty. Neither of them moved. Connie smudged the tears from her cheeks and looked at Blake with damaged, despairing eyes.

"I should have told you," she admitted. "You shared your pain and tragedy with me... I should have told you, but I swear, I didn't think my past would affect our future."

"So you don't want the paintings?"

Connie shook her head slowly from side to side and her eyes welled, making them glisten. A single tear spilled down her cheek, and then suddenly she began to weep uncontrollably again. "No," she said in a tremulous whisper. "I just want you."

She took a tentative step towards him, and then another. Blake felt his feet moving, and without consciously realizing it, suddenly they were in each other's arms in the middle of the studio, clinging to each other like desperate survivors of some perilous tragedy that had almost torn apart their lives.

40.

They made love that night with the wounds of their ordeal still fresh between them, so that they clung together with a frantic passion that was borne of their desperate need to re-connect and to heal. Beyond the physical, it was intensely emotional, transforming each touch and caress, each kiss and taste, into a re-discovery that left them ragged and gasping, exhausted in the tangled sheets, but ultimately with the bond of their relationship restored.

It was after midnight, but they still lay entwined, Connie with her head contentedly pillowed on Blake's chest, his arm draped around her naked waist. The bedroom window was open and the breeze filtered in the lulling sounds of the ocean. Connie exhaled with a deep breath of relief and serenity.

"I thought I had lost you today," she murmured sleepily, her eyes closed, listening to Blake's slow steady breathing. "It terrified me. The look on your face… the pain in your eyes. It made me realize how fragile life is, and how precarious happiness can be. I never understood before, maybe because I have never truly been happy until now."

One of his hands was by his side. She reached out for it and wrapped their fingers together. "I don't ever want to feel like that again, and I don't ever want you to have reason to doubt me."

For a long moment there was silence and she thought perhaps Blake had drifted to sleep, until she heard the rumble of his words as they vibrated in her ear. "Trust takes time," he admitted. "For me anyhow. I carried my secrets with me for five long years, Connie. And then suddenly you came into my life. But I'm not going to lie – it took a lot for me to open up – to confide in you."

She lifted her head, turned and looked up into his face. He was staring at the ceiling with his eyes wide open.

"Do you regret it, Blake?" she asked, and suddenly she had to know the answer. "Are you sorry for letting me in?"

He shook his head. "No," he said after a moment of reflection. "I feel better. I feel like the burden of sadness has been lifted. Maybe I should have sought professional help years ago. Perhaps I should have found some way to assuage my guilt and pain... but I didn't. I did the opposite, in fact, but it only made the agony deeper, the wounds harder to heal because I never gave them a chance to close."

Connie nodded gravely. "And I should have done the same," she lamented. "I realize that now. I should have told you about Duncan and about my past with him, so you would understand."

She was twisted, leaning against him with her head raised, so that her breast grazed against his chest and the nipple hardened in reaction. Connie draped a long leg over Blake's thigh and then rolled on top of him, her body still hot from their lovemaking. Their eyes were just inches apart, and her breath on his lips was warm.

"Never again," she vowed.

Blake frowned. His hands went to her tiny waist and then drifted across the small of her back, but

Connie was gazing at him, too earnest it seemed, to take notice.

"No more secrets between us," she pledged. "No more hiding the truth from each other. Do you agree?"

"I agree," Blake murmured.

"Swear it to me."

"I swear." He meant it.

One of his hands had drifted to the tantalizing cleft of Connie's bottom and he felt her squirm deliciously against him. Blake lifted an eyebrow in a question.

Connie lowered her face to his, and kissed him with the simmering force of her commitment. When she broke from the kiss, the taste of her was still wet and warm on Blake's lips. "Okay," she muttered, satisfied at last with their agreement. Then she rolled onto her back beside him and the look on her face became a sultry invitation. "Now you can have your fun, mister," she said in a soft throaty husk.

A long time afterwards, when the world was at its lowest ebb and the night was at its darkest, Blake was still awake. Beside him Connie was curled up into a tight little ball, her knees drawn up to her chest, and her cheek resting peacefully in her hand as she slept. He lay in the silence watching her – the dreamy soft smile on her lips and the slow steady sound of her breathing. There was a wisp of dark hair across her brow and he drew it away from her face with a delicate touch of his fingers.

"I love you," Blake whispered, only faintly surprised that the words would come so easily from his lips, that they did not leave him feeling vulnerable. "I didn't want to, but I do."

And then he rolled onto his back and prayed that she would never break his heart.

41.

The next morning at breakfast, Blake declared the painting finished, and then disappeared into the studio with the door closed for forty minutes. Connie could hear the scrape of the easel and the movement of furniture and she smiled at the small vanity. Blake was re-arranging everything in order to show the finished work in the best possible light – from the most advantageous position. She spent the waiting time on her phone, organizing an express courier to pick up her old paintings from the Cartwright gallery and brought north to Maine.

When Blake emerged from the end of the hallway with a blindfold in his hand, Connie's eyes grew wide with a giggle of wicked mischief.

"My goodness!" she made her eyes wide and innocent. "I didn't know you were interested in the kinky things – and especially this early in the morning."

Blake gave her a dry smile. "Do you want to see the painting, or not?"

He led her down the hallway, with Ned trailing behind. Connie walked in short uncertain steps, her hands out before her. Blake guided her through the studio doorway, and then nudged her towards the window with gentle pressure until she was in position, in front of the finished canvas.

"I'm proud of this painting," he said. "When I started, I knew the kind of image I wanted to create, and I feel the end result is as good as I could ever have hoped for. I think –"

"Blake!" Connie cut across him with bubbling impatience. "Just take the blindfold off and save the speeches. I already know how brilliant you are."

Blake fell silent, tugged at the knot, and then drew the mask aside. It took an instant for Connie to orientate herself.

And then her gaze fell upon the painting.

Her hands went to her mouth and she gasped. It felt as though the breath had been punched from her – snatched away by the impossible beauty.

The image was rendered flawlessly, capturing an essence of longing and yearning that gave the painting an air of poignant perfection. She stepped towards it, fearful that the illusion might somehow be dispelled, but instead it became even more powerful as she came closer. She studied the canvas in awed incredulity, shaking her head, feeling a mist of tears well in her eyes. It was as though she were looking at a perfect twin – a miracle of skill that gave the image life and energy and dimension.

"It's stunning!" Connie said at last. She heard the little tremor of emotion in her voice and could feel the running beat of her heart. Somehow, in some way she could not explain, the painting had the lustrous qualities of light and life.

Blake stood back, gratified by Connie's reaction. He could see in the set of her body and in the tone of her voice that her pleasure was genuine. "Don't touch it," he warned. "Parts of the painting will still be wet."

He went and crouched beside her. He snatched up the thick-rimmed glasses from his paint table and they stood shoulder-to-shoulder for many quiet minutes, inspecting every inch of the canvas.

Blake's eyes were critical, looking for small flaws. Connie's eyes were wide with head-shaking awe.

"It's like you captured the essence of me – my soul," Connie said in a husk. "But she's too beautiful to be me, Blake. The woman in your painting – she's so perfect, so utterly real with emotion and grace and... and all the qualities that I don't have. But she *looks* like me..." Connie fell into a wondrous silence for a long moment as though grappling to understand how the figure in the painting could be a mirror of her, and yet evoke so many feelings and subtle qualities in just her expression, her presence. "How did you do that?"

Blake felt a lump choke off his breathing and fought to suppress it. "I painted you how I saw you," he said softly. "I painted you through adoring eyes, Connie."

She snapped her head around – their faces were just inches apart, and Blake saw the deep swirl of sentiment move like a passing shadow behind her gaze.

"It's the best thing you have ever painted," Connie whispered, the words said thick with her own disbelief that such a thing could be possible. "I thought you were the greatest seascape painter of our generation... but you're even better at portraits. Blake – this is the kind of art that hangs in museums, not just galleries."

He dismissed her praise with a wry smile, but inside he was chuffed with pride. Connie's admiration was glowing, and he felt unaccountable satisfaction. She was no critic, he realized. But she was the inspiration for the painting, and her approval mattered more than any critical acclaim.

He set the glasses down, rubbed his knuckles at his eyes to try to clear the blur. He stood up straight, went back a few paces and patted Ned's head. The Great Dane yawned, reveling in the small amount of unexpected attention.

"What do you think Ned?"

The dog leaned against him, heavy as a falling boulder so that Blake had to brace himself to hold his balance. Ned waited patiently until Blake scratched his back.

Connie turned to him from where she was crouched. "What are you going to call it?"

Blake shrugged. "Does it matter?"

Connie looked aghast. "Of course it matters!" she declared. "All the great paintings throughout history are known by a name."

Blake gave her a small indulgent smile. "Well I really haven't thought about it," he said. "How about *'Woman Standing By a Window'*?"

Connie's expression became mortified. "You're joking, right?"

"Well why don't you come up with a name?"

Connie thought seriously. She turned once more back to the painting, consumed by every inch of perfection. The rose was exquisite – so real she had the urge to inhale its fragrance. She noticed, too, how bright and clear were the whites of her eyes now, when set within the rest of the colors.

"It has to be a good name – something worthy of the painting. What about *'Woman at the Light House'*?" she offered. "How about that?" She turned back to Blake to gauge his reaction.

"Sure." Blake said. To him it really didn't matter. And then, suddenly it did. A better name struck him. "How about we call the painting *'Lady of the Light House'?"*

Connie liked that name best of all.

42.

"What will you paint next?" Connie asked sweetly.

They were walking hand-in-hand in the wet sand. Further along the beach, Ned was running with his tongue lolling from the side of his mouth. The dog was weaving in and out of the surf line, splashing amongst the waves, and then scampering away towards the rocky promontory in pursuit of gulls.

"I have no idea," Blake admitted. It was a clear and perfect afternoon. The sky was blue, the sun was warm on his face, and he was content. Connie's hand within his felt natural, and the brush of her hips and shoulders against him as they walked along the hard wet waterline was intimate.

"What about a still life?" Connie swept the breeze-blown hair from her face and looked up into his eyes. "Every great master of the past painted still life. Maybe you should give it a try."

Blake looked bemused. "You mean pieces of fruit?"

"It doesn't have to be fruit," Connie frowned. "What about silverware, or different pieces of glass? I'm trying to think about the kind of things that would give you a new challenge – objects that would stretch your ability."

Blake suddenly laughed. "I knew another artist who painted still life," he said suddenly. "He painted from life – no reference photos, but he was also damned slow at his craft, so he went and bought pieces of imitation fruit. That way he could leave the setting for days or weeks without having any of his display spoil."

Connie nodded. She didn't see anything funny in the tale. "That makes good sense..." she said, the words lifting her voice into a kind of question.

"In theory, it did," Blake was still smiling. "But he was a realism painter, just like me – and pretty good at what he did. He painted the pieces so well that the critics complained his fruit looked too plastic."

They laughed together, the sound echoing along the lonely beach and carried on the gentle breeze. Blake slipped his arm around Connie's waist and pulled her a little closer.

"Would you think about painting a still life if I asked Thad to bring some real fruit, next time he makes a grocery delivery?" Connie persisted, bringing the conversation back on point.

Blake nodded without any conviction. He had slain his dragon. He had made a painting that was perfect in his eyes, and he realized then that there were no worlds left he wanted to conquer. The portrait had been his last painting.

"Maybe," he said without interest. "But right now I'm happy to spend time in the sun with you. Painting can wait. I don't have any plans for what lies ahead."

Connie stopped on the sand, her expression piqued. "Didn't the last couple of weeks inspire you again, Blake?" she sounded incredulous. "Didn't you feel the old thrill of having your skills come back to you, a resurgence in your passion for painting?"

Blake became serious. They were standing within the embrace of each other's arms, the sand between their toes and the lapping hiss of spent waves running over their feet. He gazed into her eyes.

"No," he said, and she could see that he meant it. "Connie, my vision is going, faster than I thought. I wasn't inspired to paint again. That's not why I made the portrait. I wanted redemption, not a new career."

"But you're so brilliant!" she protested. "Can't you see that it's a waste of your gift if you don't continue to paint?"

He shook his head. "Not once in those two weeks did I allow myself to get excited about art again," he said without tone or timbre in his voice. "Because I knew it would be futile, Connie. How many blind artists are there in the world?"

"There must be some."

"Name one. Name a famous one."

Of course, she couldn't.

43.

Connie and Blake were on the beach together two days later when the unexpected sound of a truck's diesel engine made them both look up towards the house in curious surprise.

They glanced at each other – it wasn't delivery day from the grocery store – and then they went sprinting up across the hot sand with Ned streaking away ahead of them, his bark like a boom of thunder.

It turned into a race, and Connie won by a couple of paces.

They pulled up, gasping and laughing before a medium-sized delivery truck, its engine still belching diesel exhaust. A dazed driver in a blue sweat-stained uniform climbed down from the cab. He was holding a clipboard and wore the harried, slightly bewildered expression of a man who had driven towards the ends of the earth – and finally found it.

He pushed the cap he was wearing to the back of his head.

"I am looking for Miss Connie Dixon."

Blake stepped forward. "That's me," he said with a straight face. Connie punched him on the arm.

The man went to the back of the truck and carried a cardboard box to Connie. "From New York," the driver said and then squinted at his clipboard. "Cartwright Gallery. I'll need you to sign for the delivery."

Blake carried the box inside for her and set it on the living room floor. He went into the kitchen, found a pair of scissors, and came back brandishing them. Connie flung her body over the box as though he was about to do murder.

"No!" she squealed. "You can't see my paintings."

Blake stopped dead. "You're kidding, right?"

"No, I am most certainly not," Connie clutched the box protectively to her. "They're not good enough for you to see. They were painted years ago."

"But Connie, I want to see them."

She shook her head. "I would be too embarrassed."

Blake set the scissors down. "I showed you all of my old paintings," he said reasonably. "It's only fair that you should show me your work."

"Blake, we're in different leagues!" Connie's voice became a whine. "I was an amateur. I didn't have your skill, your experience, or your knowledge. My work compared to yours would be…"

"Leave me to be the judge of that," Blake softened his voice, like he was trying to gently coax a jumper off a ledge. "And besides," he laid down his trump card, wrapping his tongue gloatingly around his next words, "you promised there would be no more secrets between us, remember?"

Connie capitulated with a groan of despair. She made a sad face, one last silent plea for mercy. Blake shook his head with a half-smile on his lips.

"Okay," she pouted. "But let me take them into the studio and arrange them. When I have them displayed, I will call out to you."

She went down the corridor and slammed the door to the studio closed behind her. Blake paced across the floor like an impatient parent in a waiting room, and it was almost an hour before he heard the faint strain of her voice, a conflict of excitement and trepidation. He went towards the studio and stopped dramatically in the doorway.

There were a dozen small paintings on display, each one about a foot square. Connie had set two of them side-by-side on the easel's crossbar, and a couple more against the window. The rest were dispersed around the studio walls. None of the paintings were framed.

Connie stood in the middle of the floor, her arms folded across her chest and her bottom lip trapped between her teeth. She watched Blake's face closely, and he realized she was anxiously reading his expression.

He went slowly towards the two paintings that she had displayed on the easel. One was a still life, with a bowl of grapes in the center of the canvas. Behind the bowl he could see the folds of a curtain. He picked up his glasses, set them on the end of his nose, then turned his attention to the adjoining piece. It was a painting of a seascape – a single wave curling out of the ocean with a foaming white crest. Blurred into the far distance, seeming to float on the horizon line, was a non-descript headland. Blake folded his glasses and slipped them into his shirt pocket.

He went around the room, looking at the rest of Connie's paintings. His expression was rigid, his gaze sweeping over each piece, then coming back again as he inspected them more carefully. At last, Connie could stand the strain of his silence not a minute longer.

"Well?" she gasped, as if she had been holding her breath. "Tell me what you think, and don't spare my feelings. I don't want you to be nice to me, I want you to be honest."

Blake looked at her sharply. "You really want me to be honest?"

"Yes," Connie said firmly, and then added in a meek, faltering voice, "I think so..."

He intimidated her. He was Blake McGrath, the finest artist in the world and by far the most successful realism painter she had ever studied. He was a living legend, and suddenly the realization of his reputation made her inwardly cringe.

He went back to the still life on the easel and picked it up carefully. He peered close to the canvas for another long moment, and then looked up at Connie. He took a deep breath.

"If your aim was to paint in a naïve style, similar to, say, Henri Rousseau, I would say you definitely have some potential," Blake said carefully. "I see the same simplicity, without some of the detail work the Frenchman was known for." He set the canvas down and picked up the seascape. "As primitive Post-Impressionist pieces, then they are quite good."

Connie nodded. She didn't smile with relief, or gratitude. She simply inclined her head and urged Blake to continue.

Blake looked back at the seascape in his hands and shrugged.

"However, if you were trying to paint in the style of Realism..." his voice trailed away to silence because he decided tactfully that the rest of his conclusion was better left unsaid.

"Go on..." Connie said sweetly, and Blake was instantly alarmed. There was ice in her voice and he felt the ground beneath him suddenly become precarious with looming peril.

"No," Blake said and hung his most charming smile from the corner of his mouth. He shrugged. "Connie, art is all subject to interpretation. The way one person sees art is always different to the way another person views it. In fact it's the same with music, films, books... everyone is going to have a different opinion, and there is nothing that makes one person right, and another person wrong." Blake glanced at the studio door and tried to calculate his chances of escaping down the hallway safely. Connie was circling him and her mouth seemed frozen and covered in crystals of ice. There was a sparkle in her eyes like the pointed tip of a stiletto.

"I'd like to hear your interpretation," Connie insisted. "As the best realism painter in the world, and the darling of the critics, you above everyone else must be eminently qualified to critique my work – my realism paintings."

Blake was trapped. The slippery ground beneath him was cracking wide open into fissures. He took another breath, realizing that Connie would not be deflected.

"Okay," he said at last. "As realism paintings, they are awful."

He braced himself. Connie made her eyes wide and artless, and for a moment Blake was unsure of her reaction. He rushed to fill the void, hoping to minimize the damage to her feelings. "The difference is brush mileage," he explained. "You said yourself that you only focused on your art for a limited time. Connie, I've had years and years at an easel. Of course you can't compare your experience to mine. At the same stage in our careers, your paintings were probably better than the work I had created." He threw the compliment out and hoped she would be mollified.

Connie came towards him with a slow kind of stealth that made him nervous. There was a smile fixed on her face, but it looked perilously close to a snarl.

"Then perhaps you will give me an art lesson?" she asked with delicate sweetness. "Perhaps the great man can show me some of his legendary secret tips and techniques..."

Blake thought quickly. "Will it get me out of the dog house?"

Connie arched her eyebrows. "It might."

He nodded. "Okay," he said. "Choose an image you want to paint and I'll show you some of the things I discovered – but only if you stop looking like that. You look scary."

Connie gave a little grin of triumph.

44.

In a quiet moment of reflection, Connie realized that her own passion to be a painter had never left – the flame had still flickered. Duncan Cartwright had cruelly tried to extinguish her dream and so – with no other apparent alternative – she forsook the desire to become an artist and instead fostered a fresh dream to own an art gallery. Owning a gallery would give her the opportunity to remain involved in the industry, even if she couldn't earn a living from creating her own works.

Now, she had the opportunity to learn painting techniques from Blake McGrath, and the prospect filled her with extraordinary excitement, so that she spent the afternoon pouring through the thousands of seascape images Blake had photographed throughout his career, each picture filed and referenced on a memory stick.

Quite suddenly, the dream she had abandoned sparked into flame again – not so bright that she would ever abort her plans to open her gallery – but enough to inspire her to re-explore her love of painting, even just as an enthusiastic hobbyist.

"I chose this one," she came at last to Blake and showed him the photo on her laptop. It was a photo he had taken many years ago depicting a steep ledge of sand dunes in the foreground leading down onto a golden sandy beach. The mid-distance showed a procession of waves rolling in to the shore, and then a far-off headland under a warm afternoon sky. Blake glanced at the image and nodded his head.

"Fine," he said. "Now you need to choose a canvas and then project the image."

"How do I choose the right canvas?"

It was easier for him to show her than it was to explain. She trailed him back down the hallway and into the studio. Blake went to the rack and pulled out two different-sized canvases. They had both been painted orange.

"Horizontal, or square?" he held them up.

"Horizontal," Connie decided. The canvas she had selected was about two feet wide and perhaps sixteen inches high.

Blake gave her the canvas, put the other back into the rack, and then noticed the perplexed look on Connie's face when he turned back to her. She was sliding her hand over the canvas, as if trying to rub away the orange under paint.

"There's something wrong with this one," she frowned.

Blake tapped the side of his nose conspiratorially. "Trick number one," he said and then went through a pantomime of checking over his shoulder lest anyone hear what he was about to reveal. "Canvas preparation. Five coats of primer before the orange under paint."

"Five coats?" Connie was shocked. She knew it was conventional for a canvas to be primed, but five coats was unheard of.

"Think about the harsh weave of a canvas," Blake explained. "It's like trying to drag a house brush over a corrugated iron roof. The result is that you miss in the hollows, and you apply too much paint on the high ridges. It's the same with a canvas," he explained. "I've never seen a wave with

235

a fuzzy edge, nor a boat with blurred lines. So I put five coats of primer on every canvas. It fills in the weave of the material, yet retains just enough of the pattern for the casual observer to clearly see that it's an oil on canvas. What I am trying to do is to smooth the surface to allow me to paint clear crisp lines."

Connie blinked at the logic. She thought about her old paintings and went to her seascape that was still resting on the crossbar of the easel. She saw immediately what Blake had meant – yet not in a million years of painting would she have stumbled upon the idea herself.

Blake set up the projector and turned out the studio lights so that the image thrown onto the canvas would be clear and well detailed. "I'll be down at the beach," he said. "It's almost sunset."

He pulled the door quietly closed behind him and left Connie at work in the studio to trace the image. Tomorrow morning he would teach her how to paint.

45.

"If you are going to paint a convincing seascape, you must paint the sky first, and you must mix up at least three times the amount of blue sky color you think you will need to cover the canvas," Blake announced from the studio window. He was leaning on the sill, looking away towards the ocean, feeling the morning's sun through the glass, warm on his face. He turned to where Connie was sitting nervously at the easel.

"Why so much paint?" she asked. Her hands were trembling. Now she was in front of a blank canvas with Blake tutoring her, the fear of the experience twisted a knot in her stomach.

"Because the color of the sky influences everything else in a seascape," he said. "Therefore you will need more paint than you expect." He could see Connie frowning and he urged her to take a close look at the printout of the reference photo she had in her hand. "See the ocean – can you see the colors of the sky reflected in the water? Of course you can, because it makes sense. The ocean always mirrors the color of the sky, so you will need that color to mix with the shades of the ocean. And see the shadows of the sand dunes? There is a hint of blue in them, and in the wet sand along the shore." He paused for a moment. Connie was peering at the image. "And the distant headland. Can you see the blue haze of its shape?"

After a long moment Connie looked up at him, quite incredulous. "How did you know that, Blake?" she asked almost in awe. "You barely glanced at the image last night. How could you possibly have memorized the colors?"

"I didn't," Blake shook his head. "I know nature. As an artist of seascapes, you need to study nature. Those things I just mentioned were not from observing the photo, they come from understanding how nature affects the photo. If you're going to paint, you need to become a keen observer."

Connie bent over the paint table and began mixing. Blake went to the radio and the room filled with quiet background noise.

"And remember that the sky at the horizon line is always lighter," he cautioned her from the studio door. "Make sure you reflect that when you begin painting."

He left her alone, went out into the living room and sat with Ned. The dog was sleeping, barely lifting his lids open when Blake sat on the edge of the mattress and patted his head. After an hour he went back to check on Connie's progress.

She was painting the sky, working in long horizontal strokes across the canvas. He grabbed her by the elbow so that she squealed in surprise.

"Wrong!" he said. "You can't paint realism by swinging your arm like you are swatting flies, and you can't paint realism by holding the top of the brush." He took the paintbrush from her hand and showed her how to hold it like a pen, fingers gripping the metal just above the bristles. "To paint real, grip the steel," he told her the rhyme. "And to paint real, you must reduce the leverage so that you control the stroke. If you power each stroke with your elbow, it's like using a long lever – you lose control. So you must learn to power each stroke with your wrist. The closer the energy to the tip of the brush, the more control you will have of each stroke."

Blake filled in the hours walking in quiet contemplation along the beach and came back again in the afternoon. He was bare-chested. The long days in the sun had darkened his skin to the color of mahogany. Connie had finished painting the sky and looked up at him, eagerly seeking comment.

Blake reached for his glasses and peered carefully at the canvas, then compared the color to the reference photo. He nodded, inclined his head, and then stood up. "Pretty good," he admitted gruffly, and Connie felt the grin break out wide across her face.

"But you will need to understand the importance of brush stroke direction before you take the next step," Blake cautioned, and saw her smile slip just a little. "Every time you paint something you must be instinctively aware of its shape and its form, and then mirror that with the way you use the brush."

Connie had a vague understanding of the concept but the look on her face gave Blake no confidence. He picked up a paintbrush and began waving it in the air, as though he were painting on an invisible canvas.

"If I am painting waves, I paint in curled strokes because I want to replicate the dynamic of the subject," he said, demonstrating as he spoke. "And if I am painting a ball, then my strokes are going to curve around the shape, because I'm trying to replicate the dimensions and depth," he said. He threw the brush down on the paint table. "It will also help you with shine and shadow – so understand the objects you are about to paint, and try to paint them as they were formed."

Connie started on the distant headland and Blake explained the logic behind color mixing – how the greens and browns of the promontory must include elements of the sky in order for it to be rendered convincingly. Connie spent an hour mixing color and another two hours painting before she was satisfied.

"Now blur the edges of the headland," Blake said. "To create the illusion of distance. Melt it into the haze of the horizon."

Connie worked on the canvas for another hour then looked up with a sudden start. The day had passed her by, and through the window she could see the afternoon beginning to fade into dusk. She stood and yawned. She could not remember a more exhausting day, or a day where she had learned so much about painting. She turned to Blake with deepened respect and admiration in her eyes. "You taught me things I could never have understood before today," she leaned against him and lifted herself onto her toes to kiss him lightly on the lips. "Even though you were mean and demanding."

She cupped his face and kissed him again, this time more passionately, and it was not until later when he showered that he realized she had deliberately left sky blue fingerprints of paint smeared on his cheeks.

The days that followed were filled with exhausting activity for Connie. She painted in the studio every morning under Blake's painstaking tuition, and in the afternoons she began photographing his old seascapes in preparation for the opening of the gallery. Tradesmen repainted the building in Hoyt Harbor, and new lighting was installed. Finally, catalogues arrived from the printers and were sent around the world to galleries and collectors in Europe and Asia.

She tumbled into bed each night and curled up in Blake's arms, languid and contented, and they made slow unhurried love until the passing of time became a blissful blur.

After a week the painting was finished and she stood back in astonished amazement, unable to believe the work was by her hand. It was by no means flawless, but the miraculous leap she saw between the art of her past and this new painting defied description.

Blake inspected the painting critically and then smiled into her eyes with pure unaffected admiration. "Terrific," he said and picked her up into his arms, swinging her around in a circle of laughter. "You, young lady, have some serious talent."

They hung the painting in the living room and Blake took photos of Connie standing proudly next to the finished canvas with Ned by her side.

Connie beamed a smile for the camera. Her dream to paint had been re-kindled and the gallery was just a month away from opening. She was falling in love with Blake and the house by the beach had become a happy home, still echoing the sadness of the past, but now with those sounds of sorrow at last drowned out by the tinkle of laughter and the soft murmurs of loving.

They were the happiest days of her life.

46.

It was on the last day of summer that Blake woke up and realized that his world had turned to darkness and he was utterly blind. In an instant their world fell apart – came crashing down, and plunged them into black despair and devastation.

Despite always knowing it was coming – despite the steady diminishing of his sight – now suddenly Blake was shocked. He was blind, and the realization appalled him and filled him with trembling terror.

He sat up in bed, groped wordlessly for his jeans, and pulled them on. His blood had turned to ice in his veins, dread clutching at his heart so that his breathing was short and shallow. He got to his feet on shaking legs and the sound in his throat was a pitiful sob.

"Connie, I'm blind."

He heard her move on the bed, heard the urgent rustle of the sheets around her and then her sudden startled gasp of disbelief.

His words echoed in his head for long numbing seconds – and then an unholy anger came upon him, roaring and snarling and ravenous behind his sightless eyes.

His instinct was to rage against the atrocious cruelty of it. He blundered through the house, kicking over furniture and bellowing his desolation like a wounded beast. He stumbled over the sofa, groped sightless for the living room wall and clawed his way towards the studio. A glass at his elbow fell to the floor and shattered, one of the rugs slipped from beneath his feet and he crashed painfully to the ground.

Connie came from the bedroom behind him, her hands clutched to her mouth, and she was sobbing tears of distress and helplessness. She heard the torture in Blake's voice and she was powerless to reach him. She cringed against the doorway as he crashed futilely through the house.

In a spare room closet was a cane that Blake had been given by the eye specialists many years before. He groped for it now like an angry drunkard, felt it in his hand and wielded it like a sword.

"Why me?" he screamed. "Why did you do this to me? Haven't I suffered enough?" He groped his way back along the hall. He was breathing raggedly. He stumbled to the screen door and kicked it open in his wrath. Ned cowered, not understanding. The great dog slinked timidly with its head hung low to where Connie crouched against the wall, and both woman and beast were trembling.

Blake swung the cane viciously in front of him, heard it crack loud against the porch railing. He stumbled down the stairs and fell into the sand. He felt rain spatter against his head, and sensed the anger of the sky, humming in the air like electricity. He went away down to the beach, falling again and again, but each time dragging himself to his feet, sobbing in grief and anguish with each step until he was just a small broken figure on the sand, against the backdrop of a boiling grey sky full of thunder and menace.

For a day and a night Blake wandered endlessly along the length of the deserted beach while the storm winds snarled against him and the rain fell in a thick grey swirling mist. Lightning flickered in the sky and thunder growled, always far off in the distance like the sound of muffled cannons. By the morning he was haggard and drawn, his legs numb and faltering so that his feet dragged exhausted in the wet sand and he fell time and time again.

Connie had sat at the window in silent vigil and watched him, her face filling with a wrench of agony each time he had come into sight, and then following him with sad eyes until he disappeared towards one of the rocky headlands. The tide had come in through the night, sweeping the sand smooth of his ragged footprints.

In the morning she could bear the torture of his pain no longer. She went fearfully down the porch steps towards the beach and into the sickly pale dawn, with no choice but to put their love on the line.

47.

He did not sense her there, did not hear her soft footfalls above the effervescent hiss of the waves running up across the shore, so that when she spoke, the sound of her voice seemed to come from a great distance away, like an echo in his memory.

Blake looked about, blind and frowning.

"Connie?"

"Yes," she said, and felt her breath jag.

Blake's face was gaunt, his eyes haggard dark holes in his face. He was unshaven, the color seemingly drained from his body so that he looked pallid as ash. He turned away from the sound of her voice, bone-weary and drowning in his despair.

"I want you to leave," Blake said, his voice hollow.

"What?"

He turned back, seemed to gaze sightless past her shoulder. "I said I want you to leave," he repeated, trying to embellish his words with cruelty and anger. "I want you out of my life."

Connie nodded. She felt a tear run down her cheek. "Why?" she asked in a whisper, the sound of her voice so soft that Blake barely caught the word.

"Because you don't need this!" he cried suddenly, every word seething with his frustration and bitter hopelessness. "You don't need to be dragged down into this... this tortured hell of darkness. You still have your life. You're young and beautiful. Don't do this to yourself or to me. Don't stay here out of sympathy. I couldn't bear that."

"You've given me no choice," Connie whispered.

"I have!" Blake hissed. "I'm giving you that choice right now. I'm giving you the chance to get away from me, to start your life over again. God!" he clenched his fists suddenly and threw his head back to the looming sky, his oath seeming to echo against the clouds. "Please. I'm begging you. I couldn't live with myself knowing you were staying here just because you felt sorry for me."

He started to stride away, sightless along the beach. He took three shuffling steps and then stopped, turned back. "I would know, Connie," he said with raw emotion. "I would hear it in your voice, feel it every time you gazed at me... and it would kill me. I don't want you drawn down into this. You're a good soul, a beautiful person. Leave the darkness to ghosts and shadows like me. Get away while you can."

He turned away again, felt the icy chill of the breeze of the ocean slap against his cheek. He felt his feet stumble, but he steadied himself and hunched his shoulders. Connie ran after him. She clawed at his arm, and spun him around. She was weeping now, the tears slick on her cheeks, her face flushed red from the aching pain that clamped down like a heavy weight in her chest. She glared at Blake and her words were like a lash.

"I don't want to live with a disabled man!" she screamed at him. "And that's what you are right now. Not because you're blind Blake, but because your heart is hollow. It's so filled with sadness and misery and self-pity that there is no room for me. Your blindness isn't your problem. The grief that you cling to is your problem. Let it go!"

"It's who I am!" Blake shouted. "It's who I have become. Not because I wanted to, but because I was punished. You don't have to live with it, Connie. I do!"

"No!" she screamed, her voice becoming shrill and piercing. "You don't, Blake!" You can let it go, free yourself of it all, and make room for me in your life and your heart. The blindness doesn't affect how I feel about you!"

He stood, his lungs filling like a bellows with great ragged trembling breaths. She could see the fury on his face but she stood braced before the storm of it, defiant and desperate to appeal to him.

"Go!" Blake shouted again. "Get away from me."

"I wish I could!" Connie cried. "But I can't, Blake. I can't walk away from the only man I've ever met who has seen the real me – seen through me – who has seen my soul..." her voice went silent suddenly and dropped to a whisper, "and who adores me..." she repeated the words he had revealed when she had seen the portrait.

Blake felt the shock of it like a physical slap. His voice became empty, dead on his lips. "How I feel about you doesn't matter," he spoke slowly, his voice rumbling like an uneasy volcano. "This is not about my feelings. It's about your future, Connie, and all the happiness you would be giving up. I can't live with your seeping sadness. I've suffered enough pain already."

Blake had wandered down to the edges of the surf. Wavelets lapped around their feet and splashed up their legs. Connie barely seemed to notice.

"I know you've suffered," Connie's voice cracked with her frustration. "But it's time to let that go, Blake. If you want me in your life, you have to make space for me in your heart – enough space so that Chloe's tragedy and every other setback is just a shadow."

"I can't!" he screamed. "I just want to be left alone. Leave me to drown in this misery, and get the hell out of my life."

Connie's eyes hardened, and at last the frustration in her burst over the walls that had dammed it. Her face twisted into an angry snarl and she planted her hands in the middle of Blake's chest and pushed him backwards with all of her might.

The surf was churning along the shore, waves hissing and tugging at their feet as they were sucked back into the ocean so that the sand beneath them seemed to melt away. Blake staggered off balance and his arms flailed wildly for a handhold that was not there. He fell back into the surf and the sea came crashing down upon him, so that he rolled, helpless, out into deeper water.

He came to his knees, water streaming from his head and chest, his face a mask of fear and panic. The next wave was larger than the first. It erupted over his back, pushed him forward and then dragged him away again so that he went down below the churning surface, gasping and heaving for breath.

Salt water filled his mouth and scalded the back of his throat. He clawed his way, lost, until at last his head broke the surface. He could feel the sand beneath his feet, the beach shoaling quickly away into deep water. He swung his arms, flailed and thrashed, gulping huge lungsful of air before the next wave dashed over him and he was pounded back below the surging maelstrom.

He was fifty feet offshore, carried by the rip of the current until he could not feel the bottom and his terror became white and blinding.

"Help!" he screamed, his head bobbing like a cork for a moment before another rolling swell washed over him. "Connie! Help me!"

"No!" Connie stood on the shore, creeping out into the surf until it was washing around her hips, but refusing to go further. She could feel the relentless tug of the ocean like tentacles clawing at her. "Come to me!" she cried out, screaming and crying at the same time so that the words were tortured and desperate.

"Help me!' Blake retched. He could feel himself being drawn out to sea. "Please!"

"No!" Connie sobbed. "Find your way back to me, Blake! Listen to my voice and come to me."

"Connie!"

"Find me, Blake! Listen to my voice, and come back to me!"

The pain in Connie's chest was deep and as sharp as a piercing knife, so that she could feel herself bleeding with the terror and fear that clutched at her. She was trembling with panic, and the horror of all she had risked. She hovered in the waist-deep water, torn to pieces by the desperation of his pleas and fretted whether she should go to him – if she should swim out to Blake and help him back to shore. But she knew too that if she did, they would be doomed.

"Listen to my voice, and come back to me!" she called again with rising dread.

And then she whispered, "Please!"

Blake struggled to the surface and heard the cry of Connie's voice. He had time just to fill his lungs once more before another wave crashed over his head and sent him tumbling and disoriented back into the darkened churning depths. He felt himself falling, felt the icy embrace of the water, and then the burning pain in his lungs began slowly to go as numb as a fatal wound. A sense of creeping tranquility draped itself over him. The water clawed and tugged at him, the unseen current like strong fingers, until he stopped struggling and finally allowed himself to surrender. He let his last breath trickle from the corner of his mouth in a shimmering hiss of bubbles, and then the energy-sapping desperation melted from his body, and he began to float and drift.

Behind his blind eyes, visions started to swirl, vaporous as the mist but slowly filling with detail until they were so real he reached out a torpid hand, as if to grasp at them. He saw Chloe, his beautiful daughter. She was running along the sand with her ponytails bobbing at the back of her head, a shrill childish squeal of delight in her voice as he chased after her. She was laughing, her eyes enormous and filled with a child's adoration and trust. He scooped her up into his arms and kissed her, and the vision was so real he could smell the scent of her, the blossom of her breath as she nuzzled against his chest.

Then the vision vanished, replaced by other moments, each one a delight or a dread — a life played out before his eyes that ended abruptly, back in the darkness, back in the shivering embrace of the ocean.

He seemed to come alert again – cast off the shackles of creeping lethargy and his mind became urgent, his instincts for survival suddenly drumming like an insistent beat. He didn't want to die. He wasn't ready to give up. Blake thrashed in the ocean with the desperation of a man who had peered into the precipice of death – and it was there at last that he found his will to live.

His head burst through the ice-green surface of the ocean and he gasped and sobbed for breath. He flailed his arms, struck out once, and then the next wave came up behind him and he could feel the pressure of the swell as it rolled in from the ocean. He kicked his legs, his ears filled with the hissing seethe of the ocean and his face slapped by the punch of the breeze. The wave swept up and he rose above it, the pain in his lungs burning like a fire as he sucked in agonizing gulps of air.

Connie's voice came at first like a whisper, like a lover's call in the middle of a dream. He turned his face toward it, strained to concentrate. Another wave came up beneath him, but it was smaller than the first. Blake swung his arms, stayed above the surface and then Connie's voice was a little louder, a little more to his left, a little more pleading and urgent.

"Come to me. Blake!" she cried.

He began to swim, fighting to move, struggling against the clinging anchor-like weight of his jeans, his legs weary with fatigue, his body aching with exhaustion. He caught the momentum of the next wave and it carried him closer to the shore. He felt his foot scrape sand. He groped for the beach, his arms now too heavy to move and his legs like lead. Another wave picked him up and sent him tumbling and swirling towards the sand.

He came to his feet like a castaway who had survived disaster at sea. He dragged himself to his feet, stumbled on legs that would no longer move. He felt himself swaying, his arms useless by his sides. Another, smaller wave washed around him and he teetered, but held himself upright.

He took a step, then another. Connie's voice was close, rising with hope and relief.

"Come to me Blake!" she called to him. "I'm here, and I'm waiting for you." She held out her hand. He was just a few feet away yet still she resisted the agonizing urge to rescue him – to lead him to the shore. "Come to me and leave the tragedy and the past behind, Blake. Remember Chloe, but come to me free of the debilitating sadness."

He turned his face to her voice, heard the hope and desperation in her words, and wanted her with the same yearning need – the need to begin again and to be rid of the sadness but not his memories.

His fingers touched hers and she wrapped her hand in his and then went gasping and crying to him, entangled in his arms and sobbing with relief and joy. He felt her warm against him, squirming with energy and vitality and he realized at last, that her love was everything he wanted, and more than he ever deserved.

"How did you get to be so tough?" he croaked, for his throat was raw and the rasp of salt water was still heavy in his lungs and on his chest.

Connie clung to him, weeping uncontrollably. She looked up into his face, touched the sallow, ravaged hollows of his cheeks with a tender finger.

"I didn't know I was," she cried and laughed, "Until I found you and knew that you were worth fighting for."

"I love you," Blake said softly.

"I know," Connie wrapped him in her arms and held him like she might never let him go. "And I love you too, Blake. With all of my heart."

They clung to each other for a very long time, the waves lapping around them, the ocean unable to tear them apart. Over their shoulder the sun rose like a renewed promise, burning through the cloud and lighting the morning with warmth.

At last Connie leaned back in Blake's arms and gazed into his face seeking some reassurance. "Are we going to be okay?" she asked in a whisper of hope.

"Yes," Blake said. "I just need to say the one thing to Chloe that I could never bring myself to say," he husked. "I just need to tell her goodbye."

48.

At the going down of the sun, Blake and Ned walked forlorn to the beach. Clutched in Blake's hand was the last red rose. He walked stiffly, the big dog at his side, nudging him with his shoulder when he veered, until they were standing alone on the edge of the ocean.

For a long time Blake stood still, did not move. The last fading warmth of the sun spread across his back, and the cold wind that would come with the darkness was still just a soft breath.

He listened to the rhythm of the surf – the ebbing sounds of the lonely sea – and it seemed to Blake as though his heartbeat began to slow until he and the ocean were in harmony.

He kissed the rose, pouring all of his love and lament into the brush of his lips. He inhaled the fragrance of it as though to sear the scent into his memory forever.

And then he threw the flower into the foaming waves.

"Goodbye my darling girl," he said softly, feeling awkward and self-conscious until the emotion overcame him and the halting words began to spill from his soul. "Always know that daddy loves you. Always know that you are beautiful, and I have loved you deeply – loved you with all my heart."

The surf seemed to give a great sigh of sorrow, as if the words were somehow were carried on the breeze and then lifted towards the heavens. Blake felt the scald of the first tears in his eyes and he let them run down his cheeks, unashamed and somehow unrestrained by the realization that this would be the last farewell.

"You are a painting in my heart – a masterpiece made perfect by my memory – and I know one day, when we're together again in the arms of God, that you will be waiting for me and I will have another life in which to love and adore you just as desperately as I do now.

"I have cried enough tears to fill an ocean, wept over the broken pieces of my heart, but I know it's a path to darkness. And I can't grieve any more. So I'm not going to wait for you any more, Chloe. Instead I'm going to celebrate your smile in the sunshine and listen for your laughter on the wind, until we can be together again."

He paused suddenly, the lump of emotion swelling in his chest until he thought it might burst and he would not be able to continue. He took one last breath, lifted his head to the sky and imagined it was a night filled with glittering stars.

"Goodbye, Chloe. I love you – and you will always be daddy's darling girl. My little girl lost."

When it was done – when there was nothing left in his heart, Blake walked slowly back up the beach. Connie was waiting for him on the porch. She hugged him and they wept quietly together, drawing strength from the shared sadness.

Then they went inside, and one by one, Connie slowly turned off the lights until at last the old home slept, and the light house was no more.

49.

Connie came bustling through the screen door, her face flustered and her eyes just a little crazy with panic.

"Blake!" she called out, snapping another glance at her watch. "Are you dressed? The exhibition opens in two hours."

"I'm in here," he called from the bedroom.

She came down the hallway, her mind a whirl. She had been at the gallery all morning, working with caterers, ensuring all the canvases were hung and attending to a million other minor things that had demanded her attention. Now she had just enough time to change, before heading back to Hoyt Harbor to greet guests as they arrived, and the doors of her gallery were thrown open for the first time.

Blake was in the bedroom, standing, waiting for her. He was wearing a pale green dress shirt and his only good pair of jeans. Connie looked at him aghast.

"Blake, the white shirt," she said. "I pulled out the white shirt for you. I even laid it out on the bed."

Blake grunted. "I felt it, felt the collar. It felt blue to me, not white. I don't like blue shirts."

Connie almost laughed, but she was too strung out, too stressed, to see the humor. "It felt blue? How on earth can a shirt *feel* blue?"

"I have an instinct," Blake declared, like it was some cosmic gift given to him as an artist. "I understand color. So I hung it back up in the closet and picked this dark grey one instead."

Connie felt herself smile, despite herself. "Okay," she nodded. "The 'grey' one you are wearing looks fine."

She kicked off her heels, changed as fast as a woman was capable, and was ready to leave again just thirty minutes after arriving. Blake had found his way along the corridor to the studio. She chased after him, herded him out to the car with his hand on her arm.

Ned followed them to the driveway. Connie gave him a pat. "Mind the house, Ned," she said gently. "I'll take care of Blake tonight."

The big dog dropped to the ground, his head down between his front paws, and prepared himself with stoic resignation for the wait until they returned.

It was an hour-long drive to Hoyt Harbor on a good day. Connie made the journey in a little over fifty minutes, talking incessantly about the minor problems that had plagued her during the day. Blake sat tensely in the passenger seat, sensing they were driving too fast, and imagining Connie waving her arms in gestures every time she spoke.

He decided it was a good thing he was blind.

When they arrived at the gallery, the catering staff were waiting for her. Connie led Blake up the steps and into the art space. He had his cane in his hand and he went around the walls slowly and carefully, counting out paces, memorizing distances while in the background he could hear Connie arguing with a man in broken English about the food that had been prepared.

He heard the click of Connie's heels and turned his face towards the sound. "Everything all right?"

Connie muttered unlady-like words under her breath, then forced a smile onto her face. "Sure," she said.

"Where are the main paintings?"

Connie led him around the room, guiding him with a hand on her elbow so Blake could fix the location of the portrait and his best seascapes. He wished he could see the space – being in unfamiliar places like this gave him no memory reference to draw on. All he had was his recollection of the map Connie had drawn in the sand when she had first discovered the shop was available, and a couple of photographs she had shown him as the tradesmen had begun to renovate.

He wasn't yet confident with his blindness, so that his steps were shuffling and almost meek – expecting to bump into forgotten objects or unremembered walls. Connie took him around the perimeter of the gallery twice, willfully ignoring everything else that needed to be attended to until she was certain he was oriented. Then she stole another glance at her watch and squealed.

"They'll be here any minute!" she gasped.

"What about your mother and sister?"

"A little later," Connie said. Her mother and Jean were staying overnight at a local motel, and had arrived just a few hours ago. In fact it was the first time in over twenty years that locals could ever remember the town's lodging being entirely booked out, well beyond the summer tourist season. There was not a room available for miles, and

Connie was expecting almost two hundred invited guests... within a matter of minutes.

Reluctantly, she left Blake and drove the last of the catering staff out through the door with frantic waves of her arms like she was herding a small flock of chickens. She had time for a surreptitious gulp of wine – and when she looked up again, she could see faces pressed against the front window glass.

The Connie Dixon Gallery of Fine Art was about to open for business.

They surged through the open door, a hundred people at least who had flown in from the four corners of the globe, followed by more collectors and investors that spilled out onto the sidewalk. One by one Connie greeted them and Blake shook their hands until he was numb and reeling.

There were many people who had invested in Blake's paintings through the years of his career. Most of the big art money now came from Asia and Europe, and as the people introduced themselves to him, he recalled names that were familiar echoes of the past. By the time everyone had arrived, the gallery was a press of bodies, almost shoulder-to-shoulder, moving like molasses from one beautiful image to the next like adoring worshippers.

Blake stood in the middle of the gallery space with Connie close beside him. She was clinging tightly to his hand and humming with excitement. She leaned close to his ear, told him which paintings were attracting the most attention, and fended off a dozen offers to purchase within the first few minutes.

"It's the portrait that is stopping them, Blake. They can't seem to move past it. They are four deep around the painting, just staring at it like they're hypnotized."

"And the old seascapes?"

"How many do you want to sell?" she was smiling, her heart pounding with excitement. It was the ultimate culmination of her dream. The gallery was a hit.

Blake lost track of time. He felt faces pressing close to him, the enthusiasm of the collectors as thick and tangible as the stuffy air around them. They were glowing with admiration and congratulations, and Blake was filled with a sense of vindication and satisfaction. Connie's excitement was a princely reward for him agreeing to offer the paintings for show, and now he was glad he had relented. She had been right, of course. The paintings were dead objects without an audience. Now they had come to life in the eyes and minds and imaginations of all these people who had traveled thousands of miles to see what he had been capable of creating. He felt a sudden twinge of regret that his days of painting were over – the energy in the room and overwhelming approval was like a magic carpet that uplifted him, and stirred within him that hunger for art that he thought had dried and withered in his heart.

Now it was over – or was it?

Blake felt Connie untangle her fingers from his and move away from him for an uncomfortable moment, and then she was back, and he sensed she was standing close before him.

"Blake, I want to introduce you to my sister, Jean."

The woman's hand was thin, the fingers almost like bones. He shook her hand and said hello. Then suddenly he inhaled a cloud of lavender so thick that it almost choked him.

"And this is my mother, Ruth. She's been anxious to meet you."

Blake felt the elderly woman's fingers cup his face and he stooped dutifully. She kissed him on the cheek, and his eyes watered from the strength of her perfume. He muttered a welcome, listened to Connie's mother exclaim about the beauty of his paintings for a few moments, and then the crowd seemed to surge around them so that he felt an arm sneak around his waist and someone brazenly pinched his bottom. He flinched, startled.

"Speech!" someone called out, and the cry was picked up and repeated by the crowd.

Connie made a quick speech, thanking everyone for attending.

"Opening the doors of this gallery has been the completion of a dream," she said. There were so many smiling faces pressed at her that she didn't quite know where to look. "And I hope that in the years ahead, all of you will return to see new exhibitions from some of the finest artists in the world. I would like us all to be friends, and I would like you all to know that you will always be welcome here."

They started to applaud, and Connie had to hold up her hands to quell them again. "Finally I would like to thank Blake. By generously allowing me to show his lost works, and his new portrait, he has provided me with the chance to meet you all, and the opportunity to make my dream come true." She stepped away from Blake and started to clap. Everyone joined her. It was a drumming of enthusiasm he hadn't heard for years. He felt himself the center of attention, felt all their eyes upon him, and he knew he was expected to say something. He just didn't know what to say – until he opened his mouth, and spoke from the heart.

"Connie came into my world at a difficult time," he began, speaking softly, as if there was no one at all in the room. "And through her love and laughter, her passion and her persistence, she lifted me up from the darkness of my despair and showed me the joys of life again. I doubt I would be here without her..." his voice trailed away into an introspective silence for long moments and then came back, stronger, as though what he said now, he wanted everyone to hear.

"I thought going blind was the end of my art career. I painted Connie's portrait because I wanted redemption. Now I am going to begin painting again – for no other reason than without art, there will always be some tiny part of me that yearns to be heard." He listened to the gasp of disbelief from the crowd and he sensed even Connie's surprise. He had not discussed this with her because he had not expected the sudden poignant rush of passion that had come from out of the silence until now it seemed deafening.

"So on Monday I am going to return to the easel – not to paint seascapes, nor to paint portraits. I'm going to paint emotion."

He felt himself frowning, felt the expectation of the crowd, and he went on quickly because it needed to be explained – not for them, but for him to understand what was rising in his heart.

"For years I painted scenes that evoked emotion – dramatic seascapes, or beautiful sunsets across a beach – images that made people feel through nature. Now that I have lost my sight, I cannot do that again, not to my own high standards. But what I can try to do, with the advantage of being sightless, is to look inside, and to try to capture feelings on canvas – raw shapeless movement and colors that are the essence of feeling."

He sensed them coming to him, his instincts picking up on the hum of expectation, or intrigue. He waved his hand in the air, as though painting on a canvas in the sky.

"I want to portray love, loss, hope and sadness – everything we feel as people, without visible images to enhance those feelings. I want to paint pure, so that shape and color are infused with their own power, their own emotions. And I hope, when the new works are completed, you will come back to Connie's gallery – and bring your checkbooks with you!"

They applauded him until the wave of sound was like a solid thing, and he felt Connie warm against him, covering his face with excited kisses. "I knew you would paint again!" she whispered against his lips, for she was brimming with joy, her eyes alight and loving.

As a man, Blake McGrath had survived, and as an artist, he was about to make a comeback.

THE END.

Jason Luke publishes a daily blog of free romance snippets that can be delivered to your inbox. For more details visit his blog at http://jasonluke.typepad.com

To find out about Jason Luke's other available novels please visit his author page http://www.amazon.com/Jason-Luke/e/B00IB45S7C/ref=ntt_athr_dp_pel_pop_1

Made in the USA
Lexington, KY
18 December 2015